SPIRITS
AND
SECRETS

A Ghost Story; A Tale of Love and Values

BARBARA ANN PERKINS

ISBN 978-1-63814-254-6 (Paperback)
ISBN 978-1-63814-255-3 (Digital)

Covenant Books
11661 Hwy 707
Murrells Inlet, SC 29576
www.covenantbooks.com

To my husband, Gary, for encouraging me to publish my book, and my daughter, Kari, for spending hours with me editing the story and whipping it into shape.

PROLOGUE

At fifty-six, I'm thinking over my life and some of the crucial moments that may have directed my choices. Having left my faith behind sometime in my twenties, I was lucky to hold on to my moral compass, kind of. (I guess it was ingrained in me.) Comfortably returning to religion and life with focus and purpose, I guess I have ghosts to thank and a story to tell. Then again, maybe spirits had nothing to do with my decisions. The wisdom was in me all along—a God-given perception that led me on the right path. However, admitting that might take away some of the mysticism of my tale, and yes, it is filled with mysticism. I like it that way.

I discovered things that decisive summer I would never admit to you if we met in person. For one thing, I've always been a bit wishy-washy, unable to make decisions. I never thought it was in me to decide quickly and be sure of that decision. But decisiveness was one thing I learned that summer. I could do it. You would think me crazy or at least eccentric if I told you in person all that happened to me or if I shared my inner thoughts. But you don't know me, so I can be perfectly blunt with you. I can tell you everything, all my secrets.

As the years go by, 1996 becomes hazy, as if it never happened, at least not the way I'm thinking it did.

I made both good and bad decisions, but I made the choices. Viewing those summer events as a pivotal time in my life, I look back and it was.

Stephanie Beinfield

CHAPTER 1

There was no light at the end of my tunnel, only darkness and an ugly little brown logged cabin facing the angry churning water of Butternut Lake. That's exactly how I felt after a five-hour drive in a summer storm. What was I doing here? I knew why I came. Jeb and I were teachers—me, fifth grade, Jeb, business ed. He inherited a little money after his former wife died, and he decided to open a business—a sporting goods shop.

I remember saying no, yelling, "Why would you give up a perfectly good teaching job with security, summers off, insurance, and a pension to open a business?"

It raised a bit of tension in our marriage for a while. Then this summer, I offered to help part time, either work on the books or work the floor on Saturdays. Lisa, our daughter from his former marriage could babysit our three-year-old one day a week. Nope. He hired summer help. I should stay home with the two girls and enjoy the summer. Forget it; I remembered yelling. "I'll take the girls up to that lake cabin you never talk about. I'll enjoy the summer all right!" I had made a decision, right or wrong, a decision. Decision-making had never been my strong point.

My welcoming sight was two rain-whipped windows trimmed in muted yellow peeling paint looking like eyes mocking me. An added-on structure (probably housing a hot water heater) stuck out like a big ugly nose between those eyes, I mean windows. I pulled along the side entrance. I felt angry with Jeb. He told me it was a depressing place, but I was anxious for a diversion. He was never home, always busy with that new business of his (of ours, I guess).

It would be good for us when it takes off. I was angry with myself. Why should I be jealous of a business? I fumbled with the car keys and opened my door to the downpour.

"All right kids, I'm opening the trunk. Grab something and run."

At this moment, although I did have an ugly premonition, I really had no idea of the life living in those cabin walls (and I'm not talking mice!) nor did I fathom the dark secrets embedded in this abode that would start to influence my life. It looked innocent, just a bit ominous.

CHAPTER 2

The moldy odor of dampness assaulted my nose when I opened the cabin door. The rain pinged on the roof and dripped into puddles outside. My eyes, becoming accustomed to the dimness, saw a large kitchen and living area wallpapered with tiny blue flowers on a white backdrop. Honey-stained wood covered the ceiling as well as the wall facing the front of the cabin. A large bowed window with white lace curtains framed a foggy view of the lake. The way Jeb had talked, I was expecting the inside to look as dreary as the outside had, but it really didn't look so bad. I still wondered why I drove myself and two kids for five hours in a rainstorm to an old abandoned cabin that had been in Jeb's family forever. The only explanation, I was nuts.

Within ten minutes, the car was emptied with the dripping wet luggage and coolers of food lining the kitchen floor. A brief walk through revealed two bedrooms off the kitchen/living area. I fell in love with the antique honey maple dressing table in the room I chose. I rummaged through our things for a coloring book and crayons to keep Allyson busy while Lisa and I unpacked the groceries we had brought from home. At three, it was all about keeping her busy. Lisa, at fifteen, would be my help. It was she who was the first to notice something unusual.

"Hey, Steph, look at this."

"What?" I was only mildly interested.

"Really, Come and look." She persisted. "It's a note or something, right on the shelf."

"A note? It's probably someone's grocery reminder."

The note did seem to be scribbled lightly in pencil on the shelf of the upper cupboard. Years had blended the writing into the wood making it difficult to read. We looked at it from different angles wiping gently with a piece of paper toweling to remove the layer of dust that was ingrained in the letters. I turned toward the old porcelain sink to wet my towel, but no water. I have to go out in the rain to that old ugly nose thing that houses the water tank and turn on the water, all to look at a silly message or whatever some screwy person etched on a shelf! Oh well, I guess I would have to do this anyway if we wanted any water tonight. I emptied a grocery bag on the table and held it over my head as I trekked out in the downpour. Luckily, I remembered to take the house key, which I managed to get into the lock after a couple of tries. I had trouble turning the damn thing. The downpour obstructed my vision, like looking through plastic wrap. After numerous tries, the lock popped open and fell into a pool of muddy rainwater that was gathering below. I managed to turn the water on, and while I was at it, I turned the water heater to hot. Slamming the door shut, I bent to rescue the lock from its mucky death and secure it in place.

Coming back into the cabin, my paper-bag umbrella was limp and dripping wetness. My hair hung damp around my face. My two daughters stared at me and laughed. Very funny! But I could turn the faucet on—well, sort of. *Click, clank, gurgle, bang* sang the pipes, then the dam broke! Water gushed everywhere! I was already soaked, so who cared? But now Lisa joined me, her long black hair hanging wilted on the sides of her face. Of course, we both yelled appropriately and looked at each other, laughing. Water pooled on the linoleum floor making dirty puddles. The faucet finally settled down to a manageable stream, but I forgot my original plan of wetting a paper towel to wash off a shelf and instead started searching for towels to wrap around our wet heads, then wipe up the floor. Thirty minutes later, we remembered our singular task. Giggling, we wet a paper towel and headed to the shelf. I wiped gently with the wet cloth, but it smeared the letters anyway. Damn. Still, we managed to get something out of it.

It's a h ppy, sunn day. M first hole day in ur
cab n.
xing up the kitch n

We laughed as we tried our skill of deciphering.
"I think it says, I'm fixing up the kitchen." Lisa giggled.
Then there was something about moonlight and swimming.
"Moonlight swim?" I squinted at the old letters.
It was signed and dated just as clear as can be:

Olivia B. June 1951

"Olivia was my grandmother's name. Do you think she wrote this?"

At fifteen, it is exciting to discover a note from the past. I remembered finding an old brown beer bottle on the beach when I was about fifteen. It was crusted with sand and other lake junk, but it sure looked as if there was a note inside. Who was I with? Oh yes, my best friend Beth. We spent hours with sticks then broken coat hangers trying to remove the contents. We never did get much out of that bottle other than old black sand. But what an exciting hopeful adventure it had been for a while! Imagine if we had found a note! I smiled at my stepdaughter. I married Jeb when she was nine. Her mom died about six months later, so I gained a child along with my husband. Learning the ropes of motherhood with an almost ten-year-old left scant time for romance in a new marriage. She called me Steph almost from the beginning (that's what her father called me), and sometime during the next six years, our relationship blossomed. A soft rumble of thunder reminded me of the dreary weather outside.

"Of course, it's your grandmother, who else would it be?" I answered. "Pretty romantic, wouldn't you say?"

Lisa's laugh was almost sarcastic. "I can't imagine my grandmother being romantic. I mean, like, what's a moonlight swim?"

"It's like swimming at night. Wonder if they skinny-dipped?"

"Skinny what?"

"Never mind, dear."

5

"Did you know your grandmother, Lisa?"

I moved back to my job, digging in the box for another item then becoming frustrated because the shelf was full; I put the item back and slowly nudged the box with my foot along to the next cabinet watching in disgust as a small cloud of dust circled the air above my box.

"When I was real little, I remember this older lady. She was always kind of sick. I think she died when I was four or something like that. So I don't remember much."

"Jeb told me your grandmother died of cancer, so I can understand why you thought she was always sick."

Immediately, I was sorry for what I said since Lisa's mother had died of cancer as well. And Jeb and I found life easier with Lisa if we didn't talk about it. The quiet in the kitchen was thick. A box of cornflakes obscured the note as Lisa continued to fill the cabinet. She didn't look at me, and it was difficult to see her profile as her long dark hair obscured her face. Those beautiful sapphire eyes she shared with her father were intent on their job of finding homes for our boxed goods. I knew by the determined way she did her job that her mind was blocking out unpleasant memories.

"Mommy, look, I made a tree." Allyson came with her drawing. "It's just like the one on the chair." Shirley Temple curls—her feature inheritance from me as I was a blond curly head as a young child, bounced about her cherub face. My mother probably watched sadly as those curls darkened and straightened as I grew, the same as I'll probably do with her. Allyson's hazel-green eyes (also an inheritance from me) blended so well with the lightness of her curls as Lisa's blue contrasted with her dark hair—two sisters (well, stepsisters) so opposite in appearance.

"Which one on the chair?" Both Lisa and I asked in unison.

"Right here, see?"

Allyson picked up a faded blue corduroy seat cushion from the kitchen chair. Etched into the dark wood was a rather immature and tiny outline of a pine tree. Under it was a knife etching, jagged, uneven, and almost too small to decipher but every letter was plainly there.

I miss Whispering Pine Lodge

There was a note of sadness built into that simple statement. And it was so short, unlike the first message we had unearthed.

"My grandparents named this place Beinfield Pines. What is Whispering Pine Lodge?"

"Don't get any ideas, Allyson. We don't make marks on furniture."

I went back to the business of putting things away. The daylight, what there was of it, was fading away. Rain pummeled the ground outside along with an occasional flash of lightening and the boom of thunder.

"After your father decided to share some things about this cabin with me, he kind of told me the story of how it was built and informed me that your grandparents stayed somewhere in the area while your grandfather was busy building it. Your dad didn't tell me much about this place, but he did tell me that! Maybe Whispering Pines Lodge was the place."

After settling Allyson in the double brass bed that the sisters would share, Lisa and I sat to relax on the white wicker couch facing the lake sharing a quiet moment together as night wrapped us in a blanket of dark stillness. Lisa was nursing a warm coke, her long legs hanging off the arm of the chair, and I had the foresight to pack that bottle of wine which I drank slowly from a water glass.

"So, Lisa, what do you think?"

"It stopped raining."

"You're right, it did. Let's open some windows. We need fresh air."

There were tiny specks of watery light peeking through the trees. Obviously, the cloud cover was finally dissipating.

After everyone was asleep, I lay alone in the metal-framed double bed. Streaks of silver moonlight pierced through the lace curtains of the small wood-grilled window. I had opened it to the aroma of wet pine needles and muddied earth, still a humid odor but preferable to the musty cabin smell. Sleep eluded me because my mind thought of Olivia. I could feel her presence. Oddly, part of her still seemed to be living in this cabin. Because of two small scribblings on wood, I felt haunted. Stupid.

But it wasn't just the thought of Olivia that was disturbing me. This was my first night without Jeb, in a long time. I really did miss him, more than I thought I would. When I first met Jeb, he had been divorced for more than a year, having his then nine-year-old daughter every other weekend and half of all school vacations. I didn't know about Lisa or his divorce at first. I actually met him in a church group for singles. Most in that group were desperate middle-aged women looking for companionship. It was Jeb's first meeting and mine. I noticed him right away with his tall athletic build, deep brown unruly hair, and five o'clock shadow at 7:00 p.m.

The memory of him warmed me, and the missing pierced my heart. I could see him so clearly sort of slouched in the chair, crossing his feet at the ankles, and looking at me with that sly smile of his. Now, I must admit, I was the best-looking chick in the group. (I giggled to myself at the thought.) I was thirty-five, looking more like twenty-five. I was able to keep a slim figure with a new diet every couple of months that I seldom stuck to and a fair amount of exercise. My shoulder-length light brown hair with blond highlights (I had long since stopped dyeing it blond like my younger self) sort of matched my light brown tending toward hazel eyes. I never really considered myself a beauty, but I managed a small nose and high cheekbones (even though those high cheekbones sometimes, especially when I was tired, caused dark shadows under my eyes). I've had several boyfriends and a broken engagement, but no one I considered marriageable had come my way. I think it might have been because I was so indecisive about things.

It was getting stuffy in the room. I got up to open the window wider. Standing there gazing out at the stately pines standing like dark soldiers in the forest, I thought I saw, just for a second, some movement out on the sliver of lake I could make out through the trees. I thought nothing of it. Probably some boater eager to get out after the rain. The night breeze felt comforting. I let it blow through my hair, breathing in a piney freshness. It seemed to relax me. Maybe I could suspend my thoughts long enough to get to sleep. It seemed to work at first. I was tired. But then the old thoughts broke through the night.

I thought of that night I had met Jeb. The thinking brought tears to my eyes, happy tears. I blinked the saltiness away. I remembered taking extra time to dress before I left home almost as if I had a feeling it was going to be a special night. It paid off. The jealousy in the air was thick when he brought me a coffee and came to sit by me during the break.

We dated almost three months when I began to be disturbed by the fact that he seemed to be busy every other weekend. It bothered me, and I wasn't sure of asking him about it. I was undecided if I really wanted to know why. Thought I should wait 'till we get further in the relationship. We had so much fun together, seeming to enjoy many of the same things, and he was a true gentleman. (I think we went out for over a month before he even kissed me. And yes, it did trouble me a bit.) He was a good kisser, but he never tried anything else. Then I met Lisa. (The thought of meeting her was a bit disturbing to me tonight. Oh, I love her all right. It's just that it changed things.) It wasn't that we didn't hit it off; we did. The problem was that he had kept her and his former marriage a secret. I broke the relationship off for nearly a month. But my attraction was strong, and I eventually called him. Okay, I called him. I guess that was decisive on my part. (Or was that desperate? I was thirty-five, and he seemed like a good catch. Would I get another chance?) Anyway, I called him, and I'm glad I did. He seemed overjoyed and promised no more secrets. He said he had been afraid of just that type of reaction if he had told me about Lisa and his marriage.

Our first six months of wedded bliss was prefect. I felt that special warming deep inside of me just thinking about it. I hugged the pillow next to me remembering how affectionate Jeb had been. For all the passion he had withheld during our dating, he made up for it those first six months. Just the thought sent sparks through my body. I wish it would have continued, but then his former wife got a cancer diagnosis and was gone before our first anniversary. I was now the full-time mom of a ten-year-old.

My thoughts (and sleep) were disturbed this time by the sound of a motor, just for a minute. I got up and peered out my window again. The sound had ceased, but I could just make out a dark form out on the water. It appeared closer this time but so still. I watched for a few minutes as the cool breeze played with my hair. The form seemed to move slowly out of the sliver of moonlight that was making a watery path on the murky lake, and it got lost in the blackness on the other side. I shivered just a little and imagined myself being a victim of first night nervousness. But I did close the window. Not even making it all the way back to my bed, I decided it was too warm in the room with the window closed. I returned to just open it a tad and pull the white curtains together. They billowed in the breeze. Okay, I could live with that, but now, I felt fully awake. Returning to bed, my thoughts plagued me. I was recalling my first few years with Jeb. With him not being here, the memories seemed to keep me company.

Where was I? Oh yes. I was thinking of Lisa. I couldn't imagine life without her now. But back then, it wasn't so easy. By the time Lisa was twelve, our mother-daughter relationship was on more solid ground, but then the hormones of her teen years kicked in with the all the situations that tends to bring. And Jeb and I had a baby of our own. That left scant time for romance in our marriage. But I always thought it would come back if love was strong and it seemed to be.

Then came that spring three years ago when I was highly anticipating summer and time to get it together as a family. I remember how I felt then, thrilled that we could have that time together. That's when Jeb decided it would be nice to be his own boss and start the business. I guess that's when I first started feeling our relationship dwindling. It appeared to be a time element: time for his business and my teaching job, time for the house and the kids but no time for us. That's the reason I volunteered to be his summer help (the proposition that he refused).

I was missing him tonight. Maybe coming here was not a good idea. What if he didn't miss me? His side of the bed felt so cold.

Okay, enough thinking! I'm depressing myself. I'm here, and I'll make the best of it. I was now wide awake!

I turned on the bedside lamp and grabbed my book—the diversion needed to get rid of my disturbing thoughts. Of course, as soon as I unclipped the metal bookmark saving my place, it fell to the floor. I tried reaching it from the bed and almost landed on the floor myself. Bad idea. I had to get up to retrieve it. I noticed something on the wood at the edge of the carpet which didn't quite reach the wall. Moving the night stand aside and grabbing the lamp for light, I tugged at the carpet corner. My nose was assaulted with a cloud of dust, but I was able to pull the carpet back a bit. Resting the lamp on the wood floor and sneezing simultaneously, I grabbed with both hands and heaved the carpet as far as I could. It stuck in spots, but my efforts were rewarded. On the wood floor written in ink smudged only with small bits of carpet backing was some kind of a note.

told Les he died and I buried him.

Tugging at the carpet, I saw more.

Les is here more now. he took me to Candles tonite and it was beautiful.
white candles in glas cups out on the frozen lake. We watched skaters skim round them.
Olivia February '55

Wow, who died? And then, so carefree, talking about a place she enjoyed being, Candles? And ice skaters? It made no sense. Unless, unless, these two notes were written at different times. I tried moving the lamp along the edge and lifting up more carpet, but the floor was bare. The room wasn't large, but the carpet was big, covering most of the floor. Moving furniture and lifting carpet was too monstrous a feat. It probably covered an entire book of happenings, but I considered it out of my reach.

One day, when Jeb comes here with me, we could manage it. Wonder if he knows of these messages? I climbed back in bed disgusted and weary. Now I didn't feel like reading either. I shut off the lamp, but damn, I couldn't shut off my thoughts.

This was definitely a summer residence, so why were they here in the winter? And why on earth would she write messages in odd places unless Olivia did not want anyone else reading her thoughts. Maybe just getting them written helped her to cope, sort of like keeping a journal. I decided not to share my latest findings with Lisa. They were a bit too disturbing. What an unusual arrival it had been! I closed my eyes and rubbed my forehead against the start of a headache and finally the relief of sleep washed over me.

*****

Outside the darkened cabin, a pale moon peeked out from the clouds. Its position in the night sky had moved, just a bit, but it still made a white path on the gloomy still lake. The path was split for a few seconds by the shadow of a boat slipping silently through the water. The boat had been quiet for so long in the darkness, quiet and waiting. As soon as all the cabin lights were out and the windows were black again, the boat began to move in and out of the path of the moon at a quicker pace. It moved closer to the shore, closer to the little brown cabin, waiting no longer.

CHAPTER 3

Rats were gnawing the woodwork, their sharp teeth making *tap, tap* sounds around me. I'm sure they were rats. I couldn't see them. But I heard them. What else could they be? I had to get out of here! Rain, dampness, moldy smells, and now rats! Why did I come? My body lay frozen with sleep when I tried to get up. I wanted to call out for Jeb then remembered he wasn't here. Damn! The rats were quiet for a moment. A dream. Okay. I'll buy that. Relax. Take a deep breath. *Tap, tap*, the noise started again. The rats started crawling over my chest, tickling me through the sheet. Shit! I threw the covers aside and leaped from bed knocking the bedside lamp off the table. Great! Groping along the wall for the overhead light switch—*click, click*. No light! By now, my eyes were becoming accustomed to the darkness and with starlight filtering through the window, I made out movement on my bed covers. Rats! Take a deep breath. Think rationally. Could be shadows playing across the covers. I was awake. Shadows, not rats. The electricity was out; that's all. I must have imagined feeling something tickle me. Then I heard it again: *tap, tap*. I remembered that flashlight on the kitchen shelf. I stepped outside my bedroom door where I was assaulted by white flowing robes fluttering in the darkness. I let out a gasp, and the "ghost" screamed.

"Lisa, is that you?"

"You scared me. I heard a noise."

By this time, Allyson was awake yelling, "Mommy, Mommy."

I tried to swallow the metallic taste in my mouth.

"You go see Allyson; I'll get the flashlight."

I was finally in control of myself.

Tap, tap, tap. The sound echoed through the cabin.

"Mommy, Lisa!" Allyson cried louder.

"I'm coming," Lisa whispered.

Pine tree branches in starlight danced across the walls, thin skeleton-like spirits waiting to attack. Finding the flashlight, I clicked it on, surveying the kitchen with the narrow white beam over the walls against the white wicker couch around the chairs toward the door. The door, was the door handle moving? Or was it my imagination? I moved in closer with the beam of light. *Tap, tap.* Yes, the handle moved!

Dear, God, help me; I prayed. This is real!

"Who's there?" I tried to keep my voice demanding and strong. But my mouth was dry with fear, and I was afraid I sounded raspy. For a moment, a frightening silence hung in the air. Even Allyson stopped her whimpering. Then the sound of shattering glass, the tingling of small pieces hitting the floor as screams came from the children's bedroom.

How could the intruder, whoever he was, have gotten around to the bedroom so fast? Quickly, I made sure the door was locked, then I ran to the children's bedroom, waving the watery beam of light in front of me. "Ouch, damn it." I stubbed my toe on a chair. I found Lisa and Allyson huddled together on the bed.

Lisa pointed to the window. "I saw something there."

A corner pane of glass was broken, although the other five panes in the grilled window were intact. Out of practice with prayer, I still called on God for protection. It seemed to calm my nerves, if nothing else. Yanking the bedside lamp out of the wall, I moved toward the window, ready to strike an intruder's hand with the lamp base. But the narrow beam of my flashlight barely lit the trunks of Jack pine and bare forest floor. The hum of a boat motor echoed through the pines; the dark shadow of a boat with two figures inside glided in the still dark water. Allyson was hysterically crying.

"Quiet, Allyson." I whispered hoarsely. Then in a softer voice, "Whoever it was, I think we scared them away. Listen. You can hear the boat motor."

There we were, an adult, an almost adult, and a child, each of us too nervous to crawl back in our beds. We positioned ourselves on the kitchen floor just outside the bedrooms. From that vantage point, we could keep an eye on the door and all the windows in the cabin. We huddled close for warmth and what else? Protection? Lisa secured our pillows and blankets to ease the hardness of the floor. Talking in soft voices, keeping calm for Allyson, and trying to pretend this was a camping trip. Allyson asked for her Mary Jane doll at some point, and Lisa crept back into the bedroom to get her sister's doll. Lisa and Allyson finally fell back to sleep. I reluctantly let my head nod and my eyes close. But I held the lamp base at my side for protection. The stillness of the night lulled me into la-la land while my grip was tight on my flashlight, its beam weakening and fading as dawn lit up the sky.

CHAPTER 4

The hum of fishing boats woke me in the early morning. Falling asleep against the wall and on a hard floor isn't comfortable at any age and definitely not advisable at forty. I was sore everywhere. It took me a minute to remember why I was there with Allyson's blond curls resting in my lap and Lisa lying on the floor next to me, her long dark hair obscuring her face. I recalled the intruders last night! So it wasn't just a bad dream. I carefully lifted Allyson's head and settled it on her pillow so I could get up. Ah sun. The warm rays fell across the kitchen floor. Yes! I peered out the window.

Two boats were gliding across Butternut Lake cutting into the mirrored water with their wakes. Rubbing my stiff neck, I moved from the window and opened the kitchen door letting in the warm sultry air of the early morning. My car was still there, air in the tires. After the events of last night, one could never be too sure.

"Steph, what's wrong? Is he back?" Lisa woke and whispered in panic.

"No, I was just checking on the car. Let's get dressed and find the police station in town."

I decided that was the better option than heading for home. Something about daylight, especially a sunny daylight, helps to erase fears and bring the return of logical thought.

"It's really scary not having a phone, isn't it?" Lisa called to me as she helped Allyson up from the floor.

"Inconvenient, Lisa, yes."

We left for town along forest roads with the morning sun squeezing between pine and maple and occasional birch tree branches. We came to open fields dotted with small frame homes and sparkling waters beyond them. The sunlight felt warm and welcoming as it filtered through the car windows, and it definitely added a cheery note to help melt the fears of the night.

Hemlock Bay, Population 1700, the sign read. I turned onto Main Street which ran the length of the peninsula on which Hemlock Bay stood. It was a wide street surrounded with municipal buildings and stores with apartments above them, a theater, and two churches with steeples poking the sapphire sky, and a small grocery store. Short side streets broke the pattern running on both sides to a waiting lake. I would later learn that the lake on my left was Whispering Pine Lake while the one on my right was called Hemlock. The town owed its name to a small bay formed at the tip of the town right before the two lakes merged. I breathed a sigh of relief at entering civilization. The rising sun was illuminating the sky with yellow rays behind the small post office, its flag waving in the morning breeze. Next, the library, then the fire and police building, its white brick was looking stark clean with the morning light behind it. It could have been any normal morning except for one strange thing: not one person or car was on the street.

"It looks like a ghost town," Lisa remarked.

My thoughts exactly. I wondered what time it was. I left my watch on the bedroom dresser in my haste to get going.

I pulled into the small parking lot on the side of the fire and police building. I was the only car in the lot, and the building showed no signs of life. Finding the glass door locked to my pull, I tapped on the window. No answer. Not knowing what else to do, I climbed back into my car, prepared to wait.

"Mommy, I'm hungry."

Allyson was now fully awake and started whining from the back seat.

"Lisa, how about you? Are you hungry? Maybe we could find a restaurant open and maybe we'll find where all the people in this town have gone."

"I'm not really hungry," Lisa mumbled.

"Well, it's probably early. But I could use some coffee."

I ran my tongue over my sticky teeth, wishing I had taken the time to brush. We all probably looked bedraggled. Pulling out of the lot, we continued north toward Hemlock Point. The waters of the surrounding lakes could be seen between the buildings on both sides of the peninsula. The sun now sparkled in the storefront windows on the opposite side of the street giving the area a comforting warm glow but also causing eyestrain. Wished I had brought my sunglasses. Still, no people, no cars. Our first sign of civilization came through the sense of smell—the yeasty aroma of fresh baked bread and the pungent whiff of frying grease. Next sign of life was a long row of parked cars, empty but purposely parked on the side of the road.

"I smell breakfast," Allyson chimed from the back seat.

A white wooden building stood on the street with two large windows, one boasting The Bakery open 5:00 a.m. to 2:00 p.m. daily stenciled on the glass and the other with a pink and white stripped awning overhead advertising The Peppermint Ice Cream Shoppe. Paper cones and colorful ice cream circles streamed down that window and next to it was a door with a hanging *Closed* sign. We had found the population of Hemlock Bay on the bakery side!

"Une Boulangerie," Lisa chimed from the back seat, practicing her high school French. It was her favorite French word.

"The Bakery," I responded with a smile, "I think the whole town is here. Must be one popular place."

"I'm just happy we found civilization. I didn't like feeling like I was in *The Twilight Zone*." Lisa giggled behind me.

A side wall inside the bakery held a glass counter filled with white and chocolate iced doughnuts, huge sugary muffins, fat buttery cookies, crisp brown hard rolls. Adjacent to the glass counter near the back of the room was the breakfast bar surrounded by high red leather stools occupied with the ample behinds of the residents. Pots of steaming coffee and grills loaded with hissing bacon and yellow eggs were along the back wall. A murmur of voices filled the air already soaked with the buttery odor of bakery. Two elderly customers next to an empty stool at the breakfast counter paid their bill and left, making three stools available. What luck! I ushered my small family to the counter.

"Good morning," a young waitress greeted us.

Her sandy hair poked out from under a white and green striped hat as if she had gotten dressed too carelessly. Black rimmed glasses balanced on her nose and, although not a beauty, her smile was infectious. It brightened her entire face.

"Coffee?"

Before I could answer, Allyson volunteered, "I want pancakes and chocolate milk and a doughnut."

"Just the milk and pancakes," I told the girl. Before Allyson could protest, I added, "If you are still hungry, you can have the doughnut for dessert." Then I turned back to the waitress. "And bring me coffee and a hard roll with butter. Lisa?"

"Just orange juice," Lisa mumbled. She had slumped on the stool next to Allyson, bored and tired.

"You should have something to eat, Lisa."

"I'm not hungry. I just want orange juice."

"Bring us two rolls. If she doesn't eat it, we'll take it with us."

Lisa rolled her eyes but was acquiescent.

The waitress returned juggling juice, milk, and a steaming white mug.

"When does the police station open?" I asked as I took a drink of the hot strong coffee.

The girl glanced behind her at the wall clock in the shape of a baker's hat. It read 6:40.

"Oh, in about twenty minutes, give or take. In fact, the chief is seating right there having his breakfast." Her head tilted toward an opening at the end of the counter that led into a rather long dining room. Double hung windows ran prolifically along the back wall of the room open to a spectacular view of Whispering Pine Lake, washing the entire room in warm golden light. My eyes followed to a small table by a side window where a tanned, strapping young man with sun bleached hair looking more like a summer camp life guard than the "law" was busy stuffing eggs into his mouth.

"You mean that blond guy over there?"

"Yup, we do have good-looking law enforcement here. Makes you want to get caught doing something bad." The waitress gave Lisa a knowing wink and moved down the counter to fill coffee cups.

"You two wait here." I took my mug and walked over to the police chief's table wondering if this lifeguard type would be able to help. "Excuse me."

A tanned, weathered face, with evenly set eyes the color of root beer, stared up at me. I noticed his perfectly ironed light blue shirt, silver badge on the pocket proudly displayed the profession. His eyes glistened with interest yet showed the wisdom of someone more mature than a camp director. Only the wisps of sun-bleached hair gracing his sturdy tanned forehead made him appear younger from afar. I was instantly relieved that he appeared more mature than I originally thought. He stopped chewing long enough to break into a dazzling smile; half rising from his chair, he indicated the chair opposite him as a jester for me to sit.

"You certainly are excused. Please have a seat. I hate eating alone."

I felt a bit self-conscious at first, but I brushed the feeling aside as foolish. I was a grown woman on a mission, and I sat down with determination to conduct my business.

"Someone tried to break into our cabin last night."

"Well, good morning to you too. Now what was this about a break-in?"

"An almost break-in"

He smiled a dazzling smile and took another bite of egg, making me wait impatiently. "Hmm, an almost break-in. That's interesting. Go on." He took a slow drink of coffee.

"Yes, an almost break-in, which is just as bad as a real break-in when you have scared children and you spend the rest of the night in fear."

He put his coffee cup down slowly and sat back with arms folded, giving me that "once-over" look that, from my experience, indicated physical interest. It was "the look" Jeb had given me so often in the beginning of our relationship.

"Okay, go on" was all he said but with that same secret smile Jeb had always used with me—a humoring smile.

Not overly concerned, I thought. *Probably thinks I'm a hysterical female.* I wanted to shove those eggs down his gorgeous throat, but I pulled myself together. I needed his help.

"I think they left in a boat. But they scared us to death and somehow managed to shut off the electricity. Oh, and they broke a window," I added.

"They?"

He leaned forward, finally showing some real interest.

"How do you know it was more than one person?"

"Well, I thought I saw the kitchen doorknob moving at about the same time the window broke in the bedroom. And I thought I saw two shadows in the boat when they left."

"Good detective work."

And there was that smile again.

Then he rose, reaching into his pocket to get his wallet. Now what? I thought. Is this jerk dismissing me?

He threw some bills on the table then extended his hand.

"By the way, the name's Tucker, Robert Tucker. I guess I'm the law or a major portion of it around here."

I grabbed his extended hand feeling the warm secure grasp.

"I'm Stephanie Beinfield."

There was a sudden change of expression in those root beer eyes; they seemed darker for some strange reason.

"Beinfield, huh? Interesting." He returned his wallet to his back pocket as I rose from my chair. "So you've moved into the old Beinfield place."

It was a statement, not a question.

"I have to collect my children." I told him as we walked toward the breakfast counter. "Oh, and do you know how I can get the electricity back on? Either the storm or those intruders cut it last night."

I thought I'd let him know I was wise enough to consider other possibilities. His attitude had seemed somewhat condescending.

21

"I'll call the power company for you. If you contact them, they'll come on their own good time, especially out to the old Beinfield place. But I'd be happy to do it."

I had no choice but to ignore the last statement because we were now at the counter, and as luck would have it, Allyson just got her plate of pancakes. But I was left wondering what all this "old Beinfield place" was about.

"I'll go check in. When you're ready, meet me at the station. You passed it on the way out here."

I nodded.

"Wait, never mind, I'll meet you out at the old Beinfield cabin."

With that, he turned and strutted confidently out the building waving to those who greeted him.

*****

Robert Tucker walked around the cabin surveying the broken window and fingering the cut electrical wire. (It was a cut wire. I was right.) He motioned for me to join him at the picnic table. The morning was warm and sunny, just as the early hours had promised. It made the night before seem more like a nightmare than reality. The smell of pine needles mixed with the tang of motor oil coming from passing boats filled the late morning air. Lisa was occupying Allyson building sand castles in the small expanse of beach by the lake. What a gem Lisa was turning out to be. I was happy she had agreed to come with me.

"Looks as if someone was trying to scare you." Robert lifted one leg over the picnic bench and sat sideways looking at me as I settled myself on the wooden bench across from him.

"You think? I have to admit they did a pretty good job of it. But why would anyone want to scare me? I don't even know anyone here."

Robert cleared his throat as a prelude to picking his words carefully. He glanced at the girls on the beach and then back to me.

"Do you know much about the people who built this cabin?"

22

"They were my in-laws. I never met them. They've both passed on. In fact, my husband never talked much about his parents or about this place. I only recently learned of its existence."

"Is that right?" Robert Tucker raised his eyebrow.

I did not like his expression. I found it a bit contemptuous but then much of this man was. We were not off to a good start. He rubbed his chin thoughtfully as if contemplating his next words.

"By the way, where is your husband?"

"Jeb is home, in Milwaukee. He started a new business and can't leave it for long. He's planning a few weekends up here later."

"I see." There was a hint of tenderness in his eyes, and then it was gone in a flash. "I thought you might be alone."

"Really? Did I leave a hint somewhere?"

He completely disregarded my sarcastic comment. Of course, his type needs to have the upper hand.

"Let me fill you in, and we might shed some light on what might have happened last night."

I wasn't liking all his assuming, but what were my choices here? He did come out to help. I suppose I needed to be a bit more charitable in my reactions. He shifted his frame, touching my hand slightly sending tingles up my arm. I pulled my hand away thinking he had quite the nerve just because I was alone. Seeming not to notice the slight by his facial expression, he did remove his hand.

"Your mother-in-law was quite a lady. She lived here for about four or five years, maybe six, sometimes with her husband and sometimes without. She was not particularly liked in town. Or to be more specific—"

He cleared his throat again and groped for the socially correct words.

"She was liked too much by the male population which made her not very popular with the wives or girlfriends."

"Mommy, Lisa and me made a sand castle," Allyson called.

"That's nice, honey," I acknowledged back.

"Come and see it," Allyson persisted.

"In a minute, let mommy finish talking to Mr. Tucker."

Robert smiled and rose from the picnic table. "I'd like to see the castle."

He ambled over to the children, and I had no choice but to follow.

"Hey, looks great."

Allyson ignored the comment of someone she didn't know and turned to me, "See, mommy?"

I walked up next to Robert. "Hey, it really looks great."

Lisa continued to add turrets, never gazing at us as Robert crouched down to pick up a stick. He tore a piece of paper from the pad he carried and put the stick through it, placing it on one of Lisa's turrets.

"Look, a flag."

Allyson giggled, and this seemed to break the ice of strangeness. She immediately searched for more sticks, asking Robert for paper for her flags. Lisa ignored us and continued to absentmindedly make sand mounds, so typical teenager. I watched the tender scene wishing Jeb was here.

Tucker cleared his throat as if he were contemplating saying something unpleasant. He took a few steps back to be out of ear shot of the children, and I had to step back to listen to him.

"When your in-laws left, they had a baby with them, and the town breathed a sigh of relief that they were leaving."

He turned to walk back to his car.

"The cabin remained deserted for a number of years, and then it hosted a round of wild parties."

Good old Jeb and the boys, I thought to myself.

Robert chuckled at some private joke as he looked down and softly kicked a small stone from his path.

"You know, you'd think noisy goings-on wouldn't be noticed out here in the woods. I guess people come here for solitude. Oh, and the shoreline as well as the roads into this place were lined with beer cans, old bottles, and other garbage. The residents of cabins along the road weren't too happy about that."

"Funny, I don't remember seeing too many cabins as I drove up. They're all pretty well hidden in the woods somewhere. But I suppose it would be annoying to see garbage on the road."

Again, my comment was ignored.

We reached his car. I panicked a little wondering if this was all he was going to do about my dilemma.

"So what happens next? Who was out to scare us? Will they come back?"

He put his hands up. "Whoa! I boarded up the broken window pane. I called the power company. I think I know who was out here, and I'm going in to make some calls. I'll be back tomorrow to fix that window, and I think you'll be fine tonight. No worries."

"I guess I can live with that. Thank you."

I grabbed the top of his car door as he opened it.

"Can you share with me who you think the intruders might be?"

"Teenage cousins, boys. They're untamed spirits that have been involved in things like this before. I'll call them in for questioning."

I let go of his door as he grabbed the handle to close it. Turning the ignition on, he gazed at me.

"Looks like we might have gotten off to a rocky start."

"You think?"

He gave me that smile again, saying, "Trust me. I'll be back tomorrow to fix that window."

As I watched him leave, I felt a bit uneasy. He was being helpful. Why didn't I trust him?

CHAPTER 5

I called Allyson and Lisa to lunch as I set a small picnic basket on the table. I had spent the remainder of the morning cleaning up the small fragments of glass from the broken window and trying to calm my nerves. I gazed at the square of plywood nailed in place over the broken section of window and wondered if that would be enough to keep out intruders. I shuddered as I thought of nightfall, but then again, no harm had really come to any of us. The public service people came as promised, and the electricity was back on. But I was not looking forward to another night in the cabin. What were my options? The thought of checking in at the town's only motel did cross my mind. But for how long? I could go home, another five-hour drive. That was not a good option, but it was an option. Jeb wouldn't be there much, working late. And when he was there, he wouldn't be there emotionally. He'd be on the phone or sitting in front of the TV with his eyes closed, resting. I guess we could make it through another night in the cabin.

I wished I could call Jeb. He would have some wise and comforting things to say in this situation. He always did. But I decided I could handle it. I think.

I called the kids to lunch, and as we nibbled on the tuna salad sandwiches, it was evident that Lisa had some uneasy feelings of her own.

"Is it scary to fly, Steph?"

"Huh?" I swallowed my bite and drank some lemonade.

"I mean I was never in a plane before, and I'm excited and all, but I was just wondering what it's like."

So her up and coming trip was weighting on her mind, not last nights' scare. Lisa had been invited to accompany her friend's family on a trip to Paris at the end of July. As far as Jeb and I were concerned, it was her reward for being willing to accompany me north and babysit Allyson.

I put some potato chips on Allyson's plate and held the bag open for Lisa.

"No, thanks."

"That plane's not going to crash if you gain a pound or two, Lisa." I returned the bag to the center of the table. "And no, it's not scary. It's fun to fly."

"I won't fit in any of my new clothes if I eat chips, and I really don't feel like having any."

It's kind of nice to be forty, I mused to myself. I can eat practically what I please. I don't have to fit into anything tiny and tight to impress anyone. And I munched away, kind of relieved that Lisa was worried about something other than last night.

"Did you ever fly?"

"Quite a few times, why?"

"Is it scary?"

I looked at my stepdaughter, a little girl in a big girl's body. That beautiful black hair hung loosely about her bare shoulders. She was the image of a nymph in her bright red bikini sitting cross-legged on the picnic bench, never to be quite that thin again without kissing the figure fairy. Her dark hair with her dark wide eyebrows and thick lashes was her resemblance to her father. But her face was soft and creamy. I never met Jeb's former wife, and I didn't attend her funeral. We had thought it best at the time. So I didn't know what she looked like, but I imagine Lisa's facial features to be much like hers. I wondered if Lisa had inherited her jet-black hair from her mother. Anyway, the mix was beautiful on her daughter. Wonder if Lisa realizes how attractive she is? Oh, I'm sure she's looked in the mirror once or twice.

After what had just happened to us the night before, I wondered why Lisa's questions were concerning her up and coming trip rather than the recent events unless it was her way of trying to put the night's scare behind her. So I just went with her line of questioning almost glad to be discussing something other than the break-in or near break-in.

"It's a bit scary, I guess. You hear those jet engines, and you feel all that power. Then you realize you have no control. But thousands of planes take off and land every day without incident. Those pilots and the rest of the crew wouldn't enjoy their work if they thought it was dangerous. Besides, it's the quickest way I know of to get to Paris."

I was pleased with how reassuring I sounded. Truth be told, I was always a little anxious about flying.

"Right. I still can't believe I'm actually going. And I guess I owe it all to you, Steph. Merci, Madame. Did I ever tell you that you're great!"

"No, but it's nice to hear it now." I laughed. "And don't forget your dad has something to do with the arrangement we made. Now, at least, finish that sandwich."

I turned toward Allyson who needed no prodding to eat any-thing and winked at her as she helped herself to more chips.

"I want to fly too," Allyson mumbled with a mouth full of food.

*****

It was a lazy afternoon with swimming and sunning. We were actually enjoying ourselves around the little brown cabin. It was a pleasant scene.

As evening shadows began to paint the landscape, I busied myself with baking the chicken brought from home. Lisa was doing something, whatever teenage girls do, and Allyson was under the kitchen table where she built a fort for herself and Mary Jane, her favorite doll. The blanket from my bed was draped over the tabletop, hanging unevenly on all sides.

"Mommy, I found some words."

Allyson's sweet head picked out from under the blanket.

I put the chicken in the old oven, and the oven door closed with a thud.

"What are you talking about sweetie?"

"You know, words, like you and Lisa found. Under the table."

Feeling a bit foolish, I bent to crawl under the table for a look.

"Where dear? Where are the words?"

Allyson pointed to the underside of the wood table.

Sure enough, something seemed to be scribbled there. In fact, on closer inspection, a lot seemed to be scribbled on the underside of the old wood table.

"Oh, for heaven's sakes." I climbed out to get the flashlight, bumping my head in the process.

"What's up?" Lisa appeared in the doorway of her room.

"Allyson found some more of your grandmother's writing under the table."

"Like, wow, okay," Lisa exclaimed as she crawled under the table with us.

It was awkward, to say the least, the position we found ourselves in to read the writing, and of course, the discourse went from one end of the table to the other. How on earth did she write this stuff? There seemed to be more than one entry, probably written on different days in pencil, some easier to decipher than others. I moved the flashlight back and forth to illuminate the portion we were reading. We squiggled on our backs like inchworms down the length of the table at times giggling at our predicament even though the messages were anything but funny. One mentioned Whispering Pine lodge again. It seems that someone had packed a picnic hamper, and they were headed for Penny Island (wherever that was) with a picnic. Problem was, it was Olivia and someone named Billy who was doing the picnicking.

Then there were a few sentences about getting lost in the woods and needing to get back before Lester came home and making it back just in time. I guess Olivia had gotten lost with Billy. In a corner was something about bathing in a pool, with Billy again.

"Who's Billy?" Lisa asked.

There were bits of messages that had faded into the wood with time and were difficult to read. Actually, the writing under the table told quite a story. I managed to get a stiff neck and almost burn the chicken. Allyson, tired of the words, had set up housekeeping with her doll near the wicker sofa while we finished our task of reading.

Supper was consumed quietly except for Allyson's chatter. Lisa and I were lost in thought, each dreading the night in our own way or rehashing Olivia's last message. Take your pick. Lisa broke the silence.

"Sounds like grandma had an affair."

"Maybe, who knows?" I answered as I buttered my biscuit.

"Steph, what did Dad ever tell you about this cabin?"

"Actually, not much. And he never said a word until, one night, after a party at your dad's friend, Jim's house, Jim and Evelyn. All your dad's old fraternity buddies were there. Did you ever meet Charlie?"

"Yeah, I did. I remember Dad telling Mom he drinks too much."

"Yup, that's him. He kept following your dad and me around asking about that old cabin where they had a few frat parties. We kept avoiding him, but he was sloshing his beer or whatever all over Evelyn's new green carpet, so I finally told your dad to answer him and get him off our backs."

Lisa laughed. "I do remember him. He came to Mom's house often. He was so funny when he was drunk."

"On our way home that night, I kept asking your dad about the cabin. I didn't know it existed. He was so reluctant to talk about it. I asked if it was dirty, smelly, ugly, or what. Finally, as a joke, I asked if it was haunted. He said, none of the above. It's just that he had bad feelings about it, like he was never happy there, and his mom never liked the place."

"Well, Dad was wrong. It is kind of haunted, don't you think so?"

"Why? Because of the messages we're finding?"

"Well, yeah. I don't mean ghosts and goblins. But weird messages from someone who's dead kind of counts, don't you think?"

"Possibly."

Allyson, not into our conversation, actually finished her supper before us. Gulping the last of her milk, we heard from her.

"Mommy, I'm done. Can I have some cookies?"

CHAPTER 6

The following morning broke bright and cheerful with sunshine flooding the walls of the little brown log cabin—the promise of a really good day. It had been a peaceful night. I vowed to remain quiet on the subject of Olivia.

A faint motor became louder as a boat neared our cabin. The girls jumped up and ran. I followed a few paces behind as a large red motorboat with specks of iridescent silver sparkling in the sunlight pulled up and stopped on the side of our dock. The boater jumped out and tied his rig to a post. Dressed in tight fitting jeans, a white T-shirt, and a navy baseball cap worn brim in back, Robert Tucker smiled and waved to us. He greeted the girls who were next to his boat by this time, and he turned to lift a metal tool box and a brown paper package from the seat next to him. The girls were admiring the boat, and he must have invited them to get inside because they both climbed in before I met him making his way down the pier.

"Hi there, I'm here to fix that window."

I accompanied him to the cabin. The girls were giggling and trying the various seats in the boat. Allyson sat in the captain's chair, her blond curls barely reaching above the helm.

"Be careful, girls, please." I yelled. "I hope you're watching your sister, Lisa."

"He took the keys, Steph. So no problem." Lisa sounded offended.

I ignored the tone.

"Could I help?" I asked Robert. "Hand you nails or something?"

"Or something." Robert laughed. "I don't need nails, but you could hand me that piece of glass."

I removed the brown paper covering from the piece of new glass. "What do I owe you?"

"Consider it a gift from your friendly police department."

I watched him work with determination. Finishing, he packed his tools.

"Would you like coffee, a beer, a drink, or something?"

I thought I had to be hospitable after all he did for me.

"Sounds good, but what I would appreciate even more is if you and the girls might honor me by accepting a boat ride."

"Police department isn't open today?"

He reached into his pocket, smiling as he answered, "A day off, I have someone handling things."

He handed me one of those bulky black cell phones.

"Something for you to use up here. Sorry I didn't have it for you yesterday, but I trust all went well. If you have any trouble tonight, just push "star 77," and the message will come directly to me."

He seemed a bit more accommodating today, a little nicer.

"Should I expect trouble tonight?" I asked nervously as he placed the phone in my hands.

He smiled, and those luscious brown eyes melted my very being. Shouldn't be happening, I warned myself. Remember, you weren't too sure about him yesterday.

"No, no trouble expected. I just assumed you didn't own a cell phone, and I thought you might appreciate one to use while staying here."

"I do. I mean I don't. I mean I don't have a cell phone, and I do appreciate one to use while staying here." Not like me to stumble over my own words.

"Good, then my effort to right our shaky start worked."

He laughed at his own thought. I felt a bit more at ease with him. He was helpful and friendly and not as patronizing as yesterday.

"You know I'd like to get rid of this toolbox."

He turned and walked to his boat while I went inside to set the phone on our kitchen table. Back outside, I saw him standing on the pier waiting for me.

"I would really like you and the girls to join me on a little ride."

The girls had heard his offer, of course, and were horribly enthusiastic. How could I say no? I would enjoy a boat ride.

But then I remembered his feelings about my mother-in-law and thought it good to add, "That is if Mrs. Tucker wouldn't mind you picking up three ladies."

Robert didn't look at me but proceeded to grab my arm to help me into the boat. He more or less just mumbled, "There is no Mrs. Tucker."

I accepted his help and climbed into the front seat vacated by the girls as they hopped in back. *No harm*, I thought, *in a little spin around the lake.*

"There used to be a Mrs. Tucker," he continued as he turned to start the motor. "We were married about four years. Both she and our son—they were killed in a car accident."

I'm sorry."

"It was years ago, just a memory now."

"Just a memory," echoed in my mind. He seemed so nice today, so sincere, but what sort of man would refer to his dead wife and child as just a memory? Does it matter how many years have passed? Does it ever become just a memory? I was starting to trust him and like him. Now I was having some dubious feelings again. We skimmed along the lake; the sun and wind were slightly burning my cheeks, but it felt liberating. I gazed at his strong profile, his blond hair stirring in the breeze. He turned to me with a dazzling melting smile. Obviously, he had no idea. My thoughts were my own.

CHAPTER 7

At full speed, we skimmed the water sending a fine spray in an arc along the sides. Racing past other boats, whose passengers waved in greeting, racing past the shore of mighty hemlocks, Jack pine, blue spruce, and the few remaining white birch, racing past the sprinkling of summer cabins with piers brimming with sun bathers and children splashing in the water, I felt a surge of excitement. The lake was brimming with vacationers from the viewpoint of the boat, and I had felt so isolated in our cabin. It was nice to see we weren't alone. Apparently, there were cabins hiding in the woods. My fears of the night were all but erased with the warm sun and the activity of the day. Robert took us for a spin around Butternut Lake before entering into the pass. A sign bobbing on the water tied to a buoy said, "Slow No Wake." He pulled on the throttle and slowed the boat to a hum.

"You'll love fishing in the pass. It's an inlet connecting Butternut with Whispering Pine Lake. On this end, it's called Butternut Pass. And when we get to the other side, it's Whispering Pass."

We entered an inlet overhung with maple and white birch touching across the river of water forming a tunnel of living vegetation. There was instant relief from the heat as the sun filtered through the tree branches. The floppy green lily pads poked through the water, some of them sporting the closed pink bud of a promising flower. Here and there, a log brushed against the side of the boat. It was amazing how all the activity out on the lake came to a complete halt in the pass. Robert stopped and anchored explaining that it was just deep enough for some good fishing in the late afternoon.

"Am I going to fish now?" Allyson called from her seat.

"Shh, this is a quiet place. You'll fish, but we have to sneak up on them. They're hungry for our worms, and worms don't make noise."

Allyson settled back into her seat and patiently allowed Robert to fix a hook for her. He put his arms around her tiny shoulders to show her how to cast and reel in. He did the same for Lisa. I watched, feeling a pang of jealousy that I quickly shook from my head. I didn't realize how hungry I was for a tender touch. Both to my disappointment and relief, Robert set my hook and just handed me the pole.

But before releasing it to my grasp, he asked, "Do you have a fishing license?"

"No."

He withdrew his offer of the fishing rod. "I'm afraid you'll have to watch."

I was okay with that. Fishing wasn't exactly a hot button for me.

Leaning over the boat, sinking my hand into the cool clear water was pleasure enough at the moment. The boat ride that had slipped so easily into a fishing expedition.

"Why is the water so clear in the pass and so brown in the lake?" I whispered.

"The color doesn't indicate the quality of the water. It's the Tamarack trees along the lakes; they give the soil a high acid content, and the runoff into the lakes causes the brown color. There are no Tamarack trees in the pass."

"Quiet. The fish don't like talking." Allyson mimicked

"Pardon me, young lady." Robert and I giggled.

"I got something. I got something." Allyson screamed.

"Hold it steady."

Robert helped her set her rod, and feeling no give, he handed it back to her.

"Seems you caught a log."

He took the paddle from the side of the boat and rowed toward her taunt fishing line. He stood with his back to me in his pair of molded jeans, and damn, I appreciated the sight. Stop it; stop it. Erase that thought. Remember, he was yesterday's ass. But, damn, he was so accommodating today. Accommodating, yes, but something seemed off. Call it a premonition. I wanted to enjoy my day, so I vowed to try hard to erase those negative thoughts. Robert grabbed Allyson's line and, with a steady pull, released it from the snag.

"There, now let's cast more toward the rear of the boat. There are fewer logs."

Her next cast miraculously produced a catch.

"Nice bluegill."

Lisa glanced at it and then turned away. She was ending up feeding worms to the fish who refused to bite her hook, but it was so unlike her not to share in Allyson's excitement. Allyson was born two years after Lisa came to live with us, and after the initial excitement of a baby sister wore off, she became a bit jealous of the attention bestowed on Allyson. But, in the last two years, the stepsisters had grown very fond of each other. Lisa's sudden sullen mood disturbed me. Didn't seem to be just connected to fishing. I wondered if she was having second thoughts about us being with Robert, connecting the under the table messages to me. That was a forty-year-old thought, I decided. Stop it! Or might she still be nervous about her flight? Teenage girls were sometimes hard to figure out. I looked at Robert, so sure of himself as he helped Allyson with another fish. Then he caught a few fish in rapid succession.

"Could we do something else now?" Lisa asked.

Robert winked at her. "Just so happens, we have enough for a shore lunch."

He pulled in the anchor. "Time to drift through the pass and tour Whispering Pine Lake."

I asked the question that I had been toying with for some time. "Is there a lodge on Whispering Pine Lake?"

I saw the spark of interest in Lisa's eyes.

Robert ran the motor in a low hum as he steered the drifting boat through the pass.

"There used to be. It was quite the place in its day."

An older couple, fishing poles suspended, came drifting through the water in a rowboat. They waved as they passed so close you could almost touch them. We waved back.

"It's been closed about twenty years now," he continued. "But the old buildings are still there, pretty much decaying."

The end of the pass was thick with vegetation. The trees intertwined, their leaves making it difficult to distinguish where one tree started and the other left off. Truly a gorgeous sight. We emerged into bright sunshine and a gleaming serene lake. It was interesting how several lakes flowed into each other to form a chain of lakes.

"Could we go past the place where the lodge used to be?" I braced myself as the boat bumped over the wake of a lone boater passing us in the opposite direction.

"Not only will we go past it, but we'll stop and walk around after we enjoy our shore lunch."

It was fun to be skimming along the water again, the wind blowing hair away from my face.

"We're going to dock on Penny Island." Robert yelled above the din.

I turned around to Lisa who seemed to be enjoying the speed ride as much as I.

"Hey, Lisa."

She turned her swivel chair to look at me.

"We're going to dock on Penny Island."

Lisa frowned at first, as if thinking of where she had heard of Penny Island. Then a smile grew along her face as she remembered the message written under the table.

"*Tres bon*" she yelled above the motor roar.

"What?" Robert looked to me for translation.

"Means very good. It's French," I yelled.

Right, smack dab, in the middle of the lake was a tiny island dressed in shrubbery, tall trees, and long waving grass. Circling the island, we came to a small sand beach. Robert killed the motor and stepped over the side into the shallow water pulling the boat ashore by its rope. The waves washed the shoreline.

"Land Ho!" He announced.

A tiny pit, blackened by other visitor's fires, was where Robert placed his grill, and the meal preparation began. Fish fried in his cast iron frying pan was a true feast along with a few items, he thoughtfully brought along, such as pasta salad and lemon bars and brownies. All were purchased from the grocery store, not homemade, but just the idea that he thought of it surprised me. How easily the boat ride became a fishing expedition and then a picnic. Obviously, the day was turning out exactly as he had planned. There was that nagging doubt again like a pin prick in my mind. I would have been more uncomfortable with the situation except the girls were enjoying themselves. And darn it, so was I, nagging doubts or not.

After our impromptu picnic supper, Lisa and Allyson were looking for pebbles along the shore, tossing them in the water, creating ripples as Robert and I sat in silence on blankets watching the sun settle over the tops of trees.

He finally spoke. "I hope you're not disappointed that you came."

I sipped on the can of beer he had offered me. "I—we've had a wonderful time. But I can't help wondering why you brought so much food, not knowing if we would accept your invitation."

Finishing his last drops of beer, he threw the can into the cooler.

"It was such a beautiful day, I didn't think you'd refuse."

"Kind of presumptuous but, actually, I'm very glad we came. I've never eaten fish that was so delicious."

"I have to admit, my fried fish is good." He laughed. "But you haven't tasted anything until you've had my fish boil." He raised his eyebrows over those intoxicating eyes. "Or have you been to a fish boil?"

I emptied the remaining drops of my can of beer in the sand and turned up my nose, laughing.

"Boiled fish? Doesn't sound like it would quite match what I just ate."

"Don't be too sure. You are going to be in for a treat. I'll make sure you experience that delicacy before the summer is over."

"Hmm," I put my can in the cooler. "I think Jeb would love it if we could do it on a weekend that he comes up."

I felt better for saying it.

"Absolutely, just tell me when."

Robert grabbed the cooler and headed toward the boat.

"Hey, kids, time to boogie."

CHAPTER 8

There was a place on the far side of Whispering Pine Lake that looked as if it was once a beach clearing. Wild grass poked slender heads through the sand. Part of a wooden pier stood stubbornly refusing to die, jetting out into the brown water. Not far from the pier was an old boat house—white wood frame polka dotted with rot. The top floor sported a torn screened-in porch.

"There were summer dances on top of that boathouse." Robert sounded melancholy as he pulled to the side of the old pier.

"They used to bring in bands—good bands, not that wild disc jockey stuff they play now. And the food they served! Wow. We had long tables of food, kid stuff like hot dogs, potato chips, cupcakes! But then again, I guess we were kids when we went there, at least more kid than adult. We had some good times!"

The tall Jack pines whispered in the breeze as we made our way up the gravel path to the large wooden building surrounded with an upper and a lower wrap-around porch. The structure had the appearance of bygone neglected elegance. A wide rotting staircase missing a stair brought us to the lower porch.

"Careful." He warned.

Lofty gray pillars of decaying wood and peeling paint connected this porch to the one above. Massive double oak doors would not open to our pull. Our footsteps echoed as we walked around the porch looking for a window that wasn't boarded so we might get a peek of the interior while a grayed sign, Whispering Pine Lodge, hanging vertically from one nail banged against the house. Lisa and I exchanged knowing glances. It was as if we were stepping into a time tunnel, living through the messages we had read.

"This is really cool."

I walked behind her with Allyson.

"Hey, Steph, I found a window not blocked up."

Wiping away an area of dust and grime with shirt sleeves, we cupped our hands to gaze at a dark log paneled room with a massive stone fireplace at one end. There were three round wooden tables scattered around the enormous room.

"The main dining room."

I jumped, not realizing Robert was so close behind me.

"Sorry I scared you." He placed a warm hand on my shoulder.

It felt so comfortable there. I tried to deny the sparks of feeling his touch evoked. It wasn't right, and I really didn't welcome it. The hand was removed almost as instantly as it was placed. And the shoulder felt so empty.

To squelch my feelings, I talked to Lisa.

"Can you imagine this place filled with people, all talking and eating?"

"You mean like my grandma? Yes, I can."

Lisa pulled away from the window and directed her question to Robert.

"Is there a pool?"

"You know, I think there was one, in back of the building. I think it was added on, not part of the original structure."

"I'd kind of like to see it."

We both remembered her grandma's writing about being in the pool with Billy and feeling anxious about being discovered. It was like living through a story.

Allyson ran ahead and found an old bench swing still hanging from rusty hooks. She sat on it and pushed with her feet. The swing groaned with age as if it didn't want to be disturbed. Lisa grabbed her hand.

"Come on, Ellie. We're going to find a swimming pool."

"Why did this place close?" I asked Robert as we walked along the porch to the back of the building.

"It was kind of an expensive place. City people wanting to experience the Northwoods in luxury paid mega bucks in those days to stay here. Now people fly to resorts in the Caribbean where the weather is more predictable. They just couldn't keep the numbers coming."

There was an extension building onto the back of the lodge with wood planks where windows used to be.

"I think the pool was in here."

Robert tugged on the door, and it opened with a heavy thud to a dark and musty interior. When our eyes got used to the darkness, we could see the broken white tile floor, a bit grayed with age. In the center was an empty well. Not wanting Allyson to run full speed ahead and fall into the crevice, I looked to see if she still had hold of Lisa's hand.

"Where's Allyson?"

"She pulled away from me when we went inside," Lisa said. "I guess she thought it was too dark and creepy."

I went back out into the fading daylight, hearing a squeaking porch swing, a thump, and a cry. Running to the porch, I saw Allyson on the edge of the fallen swing, crying her eyes out.

"Allyson, what are you doing back here?"

I picked her up, happy to see that she was more frightened than hurt.

"I want to swing," she said through tears.

"Is she all right?" Robert sounded concerned as he climbed on the porch with Lisa behind him.

"She's fine. Just scared."

He fingered the broken chain.

"Hey, Shortie, sometimes old is not good. Things break."

I looked to Lisa, standing below the stairs looking guilty.

"It's not your fault, Lisa. I should have been watching her, not you."

Slapping a sudden itch on my arm, I saw a black speck fall to the floor. Soon, I slapped my other arm. Robert hit the back of his neck as Lisa slapped her leg. The famous North Wood's invaders were coming out to greet the dusk.

41

"Mosquitoes," Robert said. "Time to head for the boat."

*****

The sun had set behind the trees, and a few stars were visible in a lavender sky. The pass was dark, the trees shielding it from the last light. Coming out into Butternut Lake, a brilliant orange light flared behind the dark black shadow of pines along the shore. It looked as if the forest might be on fire just beyond those pines, but there was no dancing movement of flames, just a still bright orange light.

"Looks like the landing of the space ship in *The Invaders*," Lisa chimed from the back.

"My god, what is it?"

Robert stopped the motor, and the boat rocked gently in the wake.

Slowly a mammoth orange ball appeared above the top of the trees surrounded with a tangerine glow.

"It's the moon! I never saw it like that before!"

As the full moon rose in the darkening sky, it shed a path of watery citrus light across the lake. In the distance, a boat moved in and out of the bright path.

Robert had stopped the motor, smiling, while Lisa and I exchanged exclamations.

"Look, Allyson." I reached for my daughter, pulling her on my lap. "The moon made a path on the water that looks like the yellow brick road in the *Wizard of Oz*."

"Jeb and I honeymooned in Jamaica. It was the in thing to sit at Rick's cafe in Negril to watch the sun set. It was gorgeous but nothing like this. This moonrise takes your breath away."

How quickly the moon rose in the sky and appeared smaller, its orange light fading to yellow then white as it rose higher, and we made our way to our pier.

"Wow, what a magical day, Robert. Thanks so much."

He tied the boat to the pier as the swish of waves washed the shore.

Stars were twinkling in an inky charcoal sky by the time I gazed at our lone dark little cabin, and the memories and fear of night came flooding back. The children were quiet which meant they were either tired or feeling the same nightmarish apprehension as I.

"I almost forgot to tell you," Robert broke into the silence. "I'm pretty sure we apprehended the intruders who scared you two nights ago."

He helped us out onto the pier.

"You almost forgot to tell us!"

"They're not scary guys, just two wild teenage boys who are being kept in tonight and a whole month of nights."

"And you almost forgot to tell us."

My statement was ignored (or not heard).

"I'll check everything before I go."

The girls ran the short length of the pier then stopped to wait, gazing at the evening darkness surrounding our little abode.

"Are you expecting that you might not have gotten the right intruders?" I was a bit alarmed that he thought it necessary to check things but secretly glad he was doing it.

"I'm sure I got the right people. I'm just concerned about you and the girls feeling frightened." His voice was tender, and I could feel but not see his eyes looking at me. "And you do have that cell phone. Don't neglect to use it if you have any trouble. But I sure don't anticipate any."

He walked into the cabin with us and gave the place a quick tour as I turned on the lights. I was surprised at how tired I felt. He walked around the exterior with his flashlight then yelled good night and headed for the boat. We heard the hum of the motor as he sped away. Suddenly I felt lonely. I wondered if the girls felt the same; they were quiet as they prepared for bed.

"Steph, can I talk to you?" Lisa was in the bedroom doorway still clad in her jeans and T-shirt as I was putting on my nightgown.

"Of course, Lisa. What's on your mind?"

She sat on the edge of the bed.

"Do you believe in ghosts and things?"

It was such as unexpected question that I was taken by surprise.

"I don't know if I do. Why?"

"Well, if a ghost told you not to take a trip or something like that, would you listen?"

"Lisa, what on earth are you talking about?"

"I, I think my grandma's telling me not to go to Paris."

I sat on the bed and put my arm around her.

"And why would she do that?"

"I don't know."

"And how do you know she's telling you anything?"

Lisa looked almost pleading. "I found another message this morning."

"You found a message and you didn't tell me?"

I thought about the disturbing messages I had found that first night that I had not shared with her.

"Show me now. We'll see if Olivia is trying to tell you something."

Lisa took me into her bedroom. Allyson, the great fisher person, was already sound asleep even though the dresser light was still on. Lisa pulled one of the bottom drawers completely out of the dresser and turned it around so the back side was visible. Very plainly, no letters missing, in ink pen was the message,

I'm going on a journey. I will not return to
the places I know.

I will leave everyone behind. I don't want to
go. I shouldn't go. I am too young.

No one knows the loneliness I feel. Oh
Lester, why all those wasted years? It is better that
the sea should engulf me. Olivia July 1980

"This is a strange message and kind of poetic, but why do you think your grandmother is talking you out of your trip?"

Lisa sat on the floor with the drawer in her lap. We were whispering so as not to awake Allyson.

"Well, she talks about going on a trip and not coming back. And she says the sea will engulf her. I'm flying over the ocean. It just gave me a strange feeling."

I sat on the floor next to Lisa reading the message again.

"She wrote this one in 1980." Counting in my mind, "That's thirty years after those other messages we found."

"And 1980 was the year I was born. So she's talking to me." Lisa was visibly shaken.

I thought for a moment. Then a brilliant revelation struck me.

"Remember, you said your grandmother died when you were little, and she was always sick before that?"

"Yes, I remember."

"She might have recently gotten the cancer diagnosis, and she's probably talking about her own approaching death. The message has nothing to do with you."

Lisa brightened up somewhat. "Do you really think so, Steph?"

"I do. Yes, I do." I was glad to give the child some relief.

"Was this message bothering you all day?"

I helped her put the drawer back in its place.

"Yes, all day."

"Then I'm glad we could end that. I won't even ask why you took the drawer out in the first place." I laughed and kissed my step-daughter on the cheek.

"*Merci*, Steph. And *bon nuit*."

"Good night to you too, sweetie, and everything will be okay," I whispered.

But it wasn't all that okay. I had a funny feeling of apprehension as I walked back into my bedroom. It was a feeling I couldn't place. I hadn't liked that last message at all. It gave me the same feeling of foreboding that Lisa must have felt. It put a damper on an otherwise very nice day, and I had to talk myself out of those nasty feelings, foolish as they were. At least I knew the reason for Lisa's quietness all day. Poor kid.

CHAPTER 9

In retrospect, I wish I had taken that message more seriously and actually told Lisa not to go.

I was determined not to let the ghost of Olivia disturb my night's sleep. But the ghost of Olivia apparently had other ideas. My night was split into short, seemingly unrelated dreams. After each one, I woke in a sweat. First, I was floating above the bed gazing down on a familiar yet unfamiliar form sleeping in my bed. It wasn't me. The woman tossed and turned as if having a restless night. I had the strange feeling that I had gone back in time and was watching Olivia. I woke suddenly, alarmed and panicked. The blue illuminated face of the clock read 2:00 a.m. I aroused myself enough to get up and brew a cup of tea. I felt strained and nervous and sipping tea in bed staring out into the starry night would relax me.

Placing my empty teacup in the sink was when I heard baby cries. At least I thought it was a baby. Strange, I couldn't tell the direction of the cries. I walked around the kitchen, opened the window, but the cry was the same. Then it stopped. I waited a few moments then shrugged my shoulders and returned to bed. Probably an animal cry. The cry started again as I climbed in bed. Curious and a bit fearful, I went to open the cabin door and peered outside. The cry seemed to emanate from the forest, and I sure was not going to investigate in the dark. Then it stopped again. The night breeze ruffled my gown and chilled my bones. I shut the door and stood with my ear against it. No more sounds. Then as I passed the kitchen cabinets, I could hear the cries again. This was silly. I opened each cabinet. My canned goods were neatly packed like tin soldiers on the shelf. The cries stopped. What did I expect? I went back to my bedroom determined to stay in bed this time.

However, the dreams continued their disturbing influence. I saw a bright orange light outside my window. I floated to the window in time to see a fiery ball explode in the sky. Allyson and Lisa were standing in their night clothes on the pier. They were still as statues facing the lake. What on earth were they doing there? The fiery ball descended toward them, and I tried to scream a warning, but no sounds came from my mouth. To my horror, the fiery flames suddenly consumed the two girls. I woke with a start, relieved to see the light of dawn peering through my window. This restless night was finally over. But the dreams left me exhausted.

I made a pot of coffee, determined to stay awake, mildly shaking as I watched the light of morning brighten the sky. I took nervous sips from my coffee cup trying to piece my dreams together looking for a binding thread and a possible reason for each one. The fireball had to be the moon rise. But it had been so beautiful. Why had it come back to torment me? And the woman in bed had to be Olivia. Her spirit had haunted me since the day we arrived. The baby crying? It could have been an animal. Was it a dream also? Closing my eyes, I let the coffee steam rise to warm my face. The drone of a lone boat motor out on the lake, the warmth of the coffee, and the rising sun streaming through the windows lifted my spirits. It was going to be a nice day. When I rose to refill my coffee mug, the haunts started all over again. Damn that Olivia! Behind the silver percolator coffee pot, the seam of flowered blue wallpaper had loosened with the steam. I absent-mindedly tore at it a bit as I filled my mug, and it pulled away from the wall. Where the two seams of wallpaper had met, something was scribbled on the wall. In order to read it, I had to tear the half that was pasted down, prying it up with my fingernail. Guess it would all have to go sooner or later, and I'd have to spend part of my summer redoing this wall.

met Karen today. floated by the pier in her
rowboat offered me a ride.

Putting my coffee cup down, I tugged at the wallpaper ripping it further.

> We're in somewhat the same predicament.
> Her husband is in Chicago and she's alone up
> here like me. had a nice float and a good talk.
> Today is a happy day. Olivia, September 8,

So Olivia found a girlfriend, a confidant, maybe? I was glad for her. Summer was wonderful in the North, but I imagined it could get really lonely come fall and winter. The note had been somewhat cheery, but why did it continue to disturb me so?

I made a mental note to see if I could find this Karen's old cabin like we had found the other places Olivia had written about. The looking would be fun. But as much as I tried to remain optimistic and cheerful, for some reason, a gnawing feeling of foreboding grew inside me. It was like a tiny seed, barely there, just waiting to sprout.

CHAPTER 10

In 1996, cell phones had limited minutes for calls. I didn't want to take advantage of Robert's generosity, but I felt the need to talk with Jeb.

I found the card with the store number. I had never committed that number to memory because I didn't make a habit of bothering him at work, at his request. When I called (which I hated to do because I knew he was busy), I got to talk to his new gal at the desk who was very accommodating, but not knowing Robert's cell number, I couldn't ask that Jeb call me back. Her name was Evelyn; I hadn't met her. She assured me they had been very busy, which was a good thing. Finally, I did get to talk to Jeb, briefly.

"Honey, I'm swamped, which is good for business, and I really can't talk. I'm trying to get everything in order so I can get away for a few days, and we can talk when I get there. Love you."

I don't think I got more than five words in before he breathed, "Got to go, bye."

I was put off and angry and that eased my guilt at a relationship with Robert. But the wise, moral part of my brain reminded me that starting a new business was work, and Jeb may have honestly not had the time to chitchat.

Driving to town would be a nice diversion. We needed groceries; I wanted to set up a post office box, and yes, I wanted to purchase paint. The kitchen needed an uplift. (I couldn't get that wallpaper by the coffee pot to lay flat.) That wallpaper had to go. I hadn't thought about what I was going to do about the message I read there. I had shared it with Lisa, but I didn't want to paint over it. I'd think of something; I was sure.

The post office was a white frame building next to the fire and police station, which gave me a chance to check if Robert's police car was there. It wasn't. Even though I had convinced myself that I was only going to town for "things," I had taken extra care dressing. Why? I asked myself. A little much for someone used to grocery shopping in jeans and a T-shirt.

I hated to admit it, I hadn't seen Robert in a couple of days, and I did miss his company. Maybe he'd be around town, and we could stop and chat. Then guilt thumped in my heart like an unwelcome guest. I shouldn't be feeling this way. It's just that adult company is nice, a little part of me whispered. Nope, I reminded myself, we need things, and that is the only reason for this trip to town.

A lean man probably in his early forties, with premature thinning hair and a receding hairline, was busy behind the counter of the post office, our first stop.

"Can I help you?"

He gazed at me, pushing his black rimmed glasses up on his nose.

"I would like to open a post office box, just for the summer, please."

"Just for summer, July and August or June through September?"

"I guess starting today until August 30?"

"Mommy, I want a one of those princess boxes," Allyson chimed looking at the wall display of mailing folders.

I tried to ignore my daughter. I was intent on getting my mission accomplished. For some reason, the gentleman behind the counter was making me feel a bit uneasy. It was the way he seemed to peer at me above the rim of his glasses.

"We rent postboxes by the month. It's almost the end of June, but you will have to pay for three months if you want to keep it till the end of August."

"Okay, fine, June through August then."

I felt the tug on my shorts.

"Mommy, can I get one of those princess boxes?"

"No, dear, those are boxes to mail things in. We'll find something else in one of the stores."

Another customer had come in, and the postmaster seemed impatient to finish business. He slid a form to me.

"Fill this out. Use your current address and your home address and bring it back with two forms of identification." He pointed to a counter facing the front of the office.

With that, I was dismissed and I turned to the counter to fill out my form. He moved his head to look around me and said to the next customer, "Could I help you?"

When I returned with my completed form and identification, he seemed a bit more eager for conversation.

"Where did you say you were staying?" He asked as he filed the form and rummaged through his drawer for a key.

"I didn't say. I'm on Butternut Lake."

He had only gazed at my completed form before filing it.

Sliding the key toward me, he mumbled, "Number 109. Let anyone you expect mail from know this box number."

He covered the key with his hand before releasing it to me as if to say, "You'll answer my inquiries first."

But what he said was, "Butternut huh? There aren't all that many cabins on Butternut, and I know who owns what. You wouldn't be at that deserted Beinfield place, would you now?"

I picked up the key his hand finally released before answering, "Yes, that's the one."

I couldn't quite place the look in his eyes. They seemed to suck me into their deep black depths. He said nothing more; he only stared at me making me feel even more uneasy. I pocketed the key and gathered Allyson to leave quickly before any more questions, completely forgetting to mail my letter to Jeb, almost bumping into the next patron coming through the door. Once outside, I breathed the warming morning air filled with the smells of pine, yeasty aromas from The Bakery and buttery sweetness from the Peppermint Stick Ice Cream Shoppe. Helping Allyson into the car, I remarked to Lisa who was leisurely in front listening to her music.

"That postmaster guy was creepy."

I wrote (PO Box 109) in the return address of Jeb's letter and deposited it in the drive-up mailbox.

"Lisa, I'm leaving Allyson in the car with you for a while. I need to pick out some paint since I've been destroying the kitchen wallpaper."

I took five dollars out of my wallet.

"Here, buy yourself and Allyson a cone while you wait."

Lisa gazed up without answering, pocketed the bill, and I took that as a yes. Three outdoor grills with assorted price tags stood in front of the plate glass window on a small patch of grass before the sidewalk. "Jerry's Hardware" was written in big bold blue letters in a half circle across the window. Cards advertising specials were taped to the window making it almost impossible to see inside. A small bell tingled as I let myself in. I assumed the man finishing with a customer was Jerry. The top of his balding head was red from too much June sun. Wisps of grey hair made a ring around his ears. He looked at me with a smile showing teeth browned from years of smoking.

"I need some paint and brushes. I think I'm looking for a shade of blue, possibly, or light yellow."

The lone customer brushed past me with a weak smile.

"Got a wall of cards here with paint samples."

He turned to the side of his counter. "These here are your blues."

He handed me two cards each with six different shades of blue.

"And these here are your yellows."

There was one card with colors from light cream to gold.

"Blues are very relaxing but yellows, if you want cheery tones."

I studied the cards. Blue would match the kitchen wallpaper, but then I was thinking of removing it. Yellow would bring in the sunshine. I felt myself break into a sweat which is what happens when placed in a position of making a quick decision, especially with the proprietor eyeing me suspiciously. In the end, bright and cheery won out. I picked a yellow just two shades above the light cream. Jerry got a gallon of white paint from his shelf and pried open the lid. I watched him measure some color following directions on the back of a card. He pounded the lid back in place and put the can in a mixing machine. Throwing some stirring sticks on the counter, he asked me to follow him to his trays of brushes. Why I had to follow, I didn't know, for he picked the two brushes himself and brought them to the counter with me following dutifully behind. He punched the amounts into an old cash register and waited for me to write my check.

"Just what you fixing up there?"

I gazed up from the check I was writing. "Oh, I'm giving the kitchen and living room a new look, then I might be back for blue for the bedrooms."

"Will this one gallon be enough, you think?"

I slid the check across to him. "Yes, for now. Half the walls are tongue and groove wood."

He lifted the money drawer in the cash register and slipped the check inside but not without first looking at my name.

"You the one in the old Beinfield place?"

I steeled myself for "the stare" as I answered. But Jerry just smiled again and winked.

"That place could use some sprucing up. Get rid of all the bad vibes clinging to those, there walls."

I took the receipt he handed me.

"You know, I've been hearing a lot of negative about the Beinfield cabin. It belonged to my in-laws, and I feel as if I'm some kind of criminal for moving in for the summer. Could you tell me what's so terrible? It seems like kind of a nice place."

Jerry's face turned red. I had surprised myself at my boldness, but I was getting sick of all the skepticism.

"I guess nobody cared much for your in-laws around these parts," he stammered.

"But why?" I persisted.

I had been through the explanation with Robert but wanted to hear from someone else.

Jerry seemed a bit uneasy shifting from one foot to the other.

"Just strange folks, weird goings-on. Half the men in town were wrapped around that gal, Beinfield's finger, she being a looker and all."

He was saved by the bell as another customer walked in. Instantly relieved, he yelled, "Hey, Helen, what can I do for you?"

I wondered if he was one of those wrapped around the Beinfield gal's finger. He seemed about the right age. I picked up my package and, holding on to the paint can handle, turned to leave. In the window, I could see the reflection of Jerry saying something quietly to Helen, and they both watched me open the door. Strange, I didn't know if I was imagining they were talking about me, witnessing something they thought I couldn't see? Looking down the street, I saw Robert's car parked at the police and fire building. I felt compelled. What excuse could I come up with for entering the police station? Did I need an excuse? How about a friendly hi? I spied a cute gift shop across the street. Maybe we could waste some time there and catch him leaving the station. I opted for that.

Lisa and Allyson were just finishing their cones; Allyson was wearing some of her chocolate ice cream. The gift shop held some appeal for them, after I found a washroom for Allyson, that is. Lisa looked at the row of books and the glass counter filled with local jewelry, and Allyson discovered the unique toys at the back of the shop. I fingered the merchandise; my eye was on the window facing the police station parking lot.

This is stupid, I told myself. Why was Robert so intriguing to me? People did exit the station, and every time the door was opened, my heart stopped. But Robert was never one of those people. Finally, Allyson got bored, and we had to leave.

There seemed to be one interesting restaurant or shop after another, and it was lunch time. I almost missed it. In fact, it caught my eye in the rearview mirror.

"Oh my god, will you look at that!"

"What?" Both Lisa and Allyson strained to see out the front of the car.

I pulled into a driveway and waited for a couple of cars to pass then made a turn in the middle of the road.

"Look on top of that building." I pointed to the roof of The Alpine Guest House.

The entire roof was growing grass. Three large goats, legs chained to pipes sticking out of the roof, were nibbling the grass as if on a mountain top. A few tourists were on the sidewalk taking pictures of the sight.

"Wow," Lisa exclaimed.

"We've got to stop here, girls."

We watched in awe for a few moments and then went inside the quaint and colorful Swedish restaurant. Sitting at highly varnished tables, we ordered lunch.

"Just think, goats are nibbling grass above me." Lisa giggled.

I finished my sandwich and left with Allyson in search for the restroom. Eating was not one of Allyson's neatest activities. Outside the restroom door was a public phone which I used to call home because I really didn't feel I should keep using Robert's cell phone for my private calls. It had been more than two weeks since we had come North. It was Saturday. Jeb usually came home for lunch on the weekend. Maybe I could catch him and just say hi. But all I heard was his voice, "You've reached the Beinfields. Please leave a message."

Wonder why he changed the answering machine message?

"Jeb, if you're there, please answer. It's me."

Jeb was known to not always answer the phone even if he was home.

"Jeb," I pleaded. I just want to hear how things are going. "Promise, I won't talk long." Then finally, I said, "We're fine here. The girls love it. We have a post office box. Number 109. I just mailed you a letter. We expect one back soon."

I felt it necessary to say all of this because, often, Jeb left the mail pile up on the hall table. I hoped our bills were being paid on time. He was so organized with the business, but I handled the home stuff. Just hoped he was remembering to do it.

Returning to the table, Lisa asked, "You tried to call Dad again, didn't you?"

"Yes." I took a sip of my coffee, but it had grown cold. "He wasn't home."

CHAPTER 11

The night was exceptionally dark. A wind had picked up, and the little wooden windows shook in their frames. *I hope it's not going to rain again*, I thought. I suppose we could go to town if it does, and that thought did cheer me a bit. There had been no contact with Robert which made my first trip to town a bit disappointing. I had wisely decided not to stop in for that hi. And of course, I could try to call Jeb again. Allyson cried that she was scared to go to bed alone, and I wasn't sure what brought that on. Lisa alternated between having her nose buried in a book and pacing the kitchen looking for something to snack on. Opening windows brought in gusts of wind and damp piney odors.

Lisa finally closed her book and announced, "I'm going to bed."

I was glad to carry a sleepy Allyson into the bedroom. At least with Lisa there, she might stay put.

I tried sitting up to read a bit, but I got restless, and when the lights started to flicker off and on, I decided to turn in myself. That night, I lay, my mind wandering over past events in my life as well as some of the messages in the cabin that I was now sure were meant to be kept secret. When sleep refused its relief again (it was beginning to be a habit), I tried a glass of wine, by flashlight. The wind outside seemed to be playing tricks with our electricity. A few more tosses and turns and then, this time, the lights worked when I clicked them on, and I brewed myself a cup of sleepy time tea. At last, I relaxed against the pillows with heavy eye lids, but my solace would not last.

The wind died down to a gentle breeze. The sounds of tree branches stirring in the night air, the creeks of small animals creeping along the forest floor, and the soft croak of night frogs drifting through the window I finally opened. Then something else sounded through that window. At first, it was quiet, muffled, and I had to listen intently. It just mingled with all the other night sounds. But the persistence bothered me. I thought I had heard a baby crying exactly as I had heard that second night of my stay. I hoped it had been my imagination or a dream, but there it was again! And I was fully awake this time! It gave me an eerie feeling, but at least, it seemed to be coming from outside and not from my kitchen. I was tempted to call Robert, but I stopped myself, not knowing the real motive behind my call or how he would perceive it. What could I tell him? I think I hear a baby crying in the woods, but I'm not sure, and it's very soft, subtle almost. Would he laugh at my fear? I convinced myself that it was just another animal sound. Or maybe there was an actual baby crying in a cottage down the lake, and the breeze carried the sound. Yup, I convinced myself it was nothing to worry about. Finally, sleep came. But apparently Father Night had other ideas! This was not going to be a night of rest.

Shrill screams suddenly woke me. My eyes popped open, and I sat up trying to rid myself of the fog of sleep. Was this just another dream? The screams came again.

"Mommy, Mommy!" Allyson and Lisa ran into my room.

Okay, I wasn't alone in my delusions. We huddled together as the screams pierced the night air, followed by savage growls. I flipped on the bedroom light switch. The light eased our fears a little but did nothing to stop the screams. Whoever or whatever it was, it was not bothered by our bedroom light. Allyson held her ears.

"It might be an animal," I volunteered. But I wasn't sure.

I crept into the kitchen with Allyson, and Lisa close behind me. I turned on the kitchen light. It was strangely quiet for a minute. Then the bloodthirsty yelps, deafening screams, and thundering thumps started again. They seemed to be coming from under the kitchen floor.

Allyson and Lisa backed up to the wall as if they thought the thuds would break open a hole in the floor, and they'd fall through into some dark abyss filled with screaming demons.

"What the hell?"

I opened the kitchen window and peered out into the forest blackness. Not even a moon lit up the sky, and screams came louder, the growls deeper and more menacing.

"We could call Robert." Lisa stood with the cell phone ready in her hand.

Another scream and Lisa dialed "star 77" and handed the phone to me.

A sleepy voice answered.

"Robert, it's me," I tried to sound calm.

The thumps and noises were so loud that he heard them.

"Steph, what on earth is going on out there?" The sleep had left his voice completely.

"That's why we're calling. We don't know for sure."

"Might be some kind of animal. Stay inside. I'll be right out."

He sounded ready to come, I thought. I wondered if he was looking for a reason.

"He's on his way," I told my waiting audience.

*****

"I found your culprit or, rather, culprits." He laughed as he closed the screen door behind him and turned on the outside light. "Come and see."

I watched Robert as he stood by the door motioning us closer. He was the picture of an outdoors man, filling the doorway in a red plaid shirt that emphasized his tan face and blond-streaked hair.

I had hastily thrown my robe over my night shirt following the phone call, and I felt a bit under dressed. Really?

The screaming and growling continued as we peered out the glass into the darkness which had been broken with the yellow beam of porch light. Three or four animals were locked together in a fury rolling around hissing and fighting. Soon three more fat raccoons came from under the cabin to join in the brawl. It was quite the show.

"I thought raccoons were quiet little night thieves." I laughed.

"Usually, they are. But tonight, they're fighting over your garbage. Wow, will you have a mess!"

Allyson held back, not sure she wanted to look until Robert
turned to pick her up.

"Look at this shortie," he said.

She seized Robert by his neck, a bit apprehensive to get too
close to the window.

"They're raccoons," he said to her. "Big, fat raccoons. And your
mommy forgot to put the lid on the garbage can, so they're fighting
over your leftovers."

The show continued for quite a long time. The raccoons were
oblivious to their entertained audience. Finally, for no apparent reason, they ran off into the darkness, and the forest was still again.

I surveyed the littered yard from the safety of the kitchen window. Robert put Allyson down and went out the door.

"I'll take care of it for you," he called.

I felt guilty watching him pick up my garbage. I went outdoors
to help. The coolness of night felt good on my flushed face, and that
was the first time I realized the blushing warmth Robert caused in
me. The sour smell of garbage was thick in the air.

"What a mess." I laughed.

"Always keep the lid on the can."

"I thought I did that."

Robert replaced the lid and went looking for something heavy
to secure it. He returned with a rock.

"They're agile little creatures and can easily pry a cover off."

Job finished, I felt wide awake.

"Would you like some hot chocolate or coffee or something?
And how about a good hand washing?" I added laughing.

"Hot chocolate sounds good," he answered, "and so does a
wash."

I thought he wanted to stay. I felt a surge of excitement as he
followed me in. A surge that shouldn't be, I added to myself.

Cups of steaming hot chocolate and most of a cherry pie later,
a very tired Lisa and Allyson went back to bed. That left me and
Robert alone for the first time. There were a few awkward moments.

"Would you like something else?" I asked to break the uneasy silence.

Immediately, I thought the question had sounded stupid and was sorry I had asked.

Robert smiled as if there might be something else to have, but it was his secret. He glanced at his watch.

"It's almost three in the morning. I have to work tomorrow. I better get going."

With that, he rose to leave, and I walked him to the door.

I felt rather foolish asking my next question because I knew I wanted to detain him as much as I wanted my question answered. He had become so nice since we first met. His pompous ass self was gone.

"Robert, there's something else."

He turned to face me, his hand on the doorknob.

"I really feel foolish but—"

Those sensual brown eyes did their melting trick. I took a quick reassuring breath and went on.

"I could swear that I've been hearing something like a baby crying at night."

A full smile lit up his face, making me feel at first that he might be entertained at my expense.

"Don't feel foolish. We've gotten quite a few calls about it from the vacationers around here." He shifted his weight slightly. "About this time of the year, the mother red fox takes her young pups into the woods in the middle of the night and leaves them there to find their own way back. It's sort of an animal kingdom "rite of passage." The fox pups cry like babies all the while they look for their mother. It sounds mean but teaches them to be independent. In fact, it accomplishes in a few nights what takes a human parent years to do."

"I'll have to remember that."

Robert laughed with me; opening the door and turning to leave, he faced me again.

"I have the afternoon free the day after tomorrow. Would it be all right if I came over to take the girls water skiing? And you, too, if you'd like to try."

The invitation was totally unexpected. But I was thrilled and a little too quick to answer, "We'd love it."

The enthusiasm did not go unnoticed by Robert.

He smiled that darn secretive smile of his again and added, "Don't fix anything to eat. I'm going to treat all of you to my famous fish boil as promised."

Then he lightly touched my cheek with his fingertips. "See you Thursday."

I watched him drive off, his car being engulfed by the forest darkness. I could still feel the light touch of his fingertips on my cheek as I turned off the porch light and leaned against the door, thinking. I did it again. Can I honestly say that I accepted his invitation for the girls? I don't think so. But why do I feel so glad that I called him? And guilty at the same time? Walking to my bedroom and turning out the lights, I thought of Jeb and was filled with self-reproach and apprehension. *I loved Jeb, and we had a happy marriage*, I thought. We didn't see too much of each other right now, but that's because of the business and not anyone's fault. What was I doing? Oh, what's the harm? Just water skiing and an innocent dinner, and hopefully Jeb would find a way to get up north by the next weekend. I had conveniently forgotten that I asked Robert to hold off on that fish boil until Jeb could join us. Evidently, Robert forgot that part also.

CHAPTER 12

Needless to say, the girls were thrilled with the plans for Thursday. Wednesday seemed to drag by in comparison. We did go to town in the morning. I stopped by The Bakery to purchase some sweet rolls for myself, cookies for Allyson, and something sweet for dessert for tomorrow even though Robert did not specify that I needed to add anything to the fish boil meal. I sat the children at the counter with juice while I used the public phone I had seen near the restrooms. It was early, and I was lucky to actually get to talk with Jeb this time.

"Hey, Steph, got your letter. Glad you like the place."

"Yes, well, we're trying to do a few things like paint and stuff while we're here. You know, make ourselves useful. How's everything at home?"

"Oh, same old, same old. Business is good."

"So when do you think you might be up."

A pause.

"Jeb? Are you there?"

"Yup, I'm here. Don't think I can clear myself to make it, hon. At least it doesn't look good in the next couple of weeks."

"Mommy, are you talking to Daddy? I wanna talk." Allyson was pulling on my shorts.

"I'm giving the phone to Allyson, Jeb. She wants to talk to you."

"Ah, sure thing, I miss you Steph."

"Love you too. See what you can do about coming north."

I handed the phone to my daughter, not sure this time if I missed my husband or not. And that worried me. I felt a pang of guilt. It wasn't as if I had a bad marriage. We loved each other, but there just didn't seem to be time for us. First, it was Lisa, bless her heart. I did learn to love her. Sweet Allyson was born. Then he started the business. I wondered was it just the business that was making Jeb so noncommittal? Was he seeing someone? Why was he so anxious for me to leave this summer? Why did he seem to want me to stay up north? He seemed not to miss me or his children. Those sudden ideas made me sad but oddly not overly worried. The thoughts appeared to be giving me an excuse to keep seeing Robert. And the prospect of seeing Robert was exciting. I knew in my heart something wasn't right.

"Hi, Daddy. Uh huh." Allyson shook her head. "No, ah, ah. Yup. Okay. Miss you, Daddy."

Typical child.

"Lisa," I called to my stepdaughter, who was fingering through a newspaper someone had left on the counter. "Your dad is on the phone. Want to say something?"

Lisa looked up and shook her head negatively and went back to reading. When she didn't come to the phone, Jeb said, "Let me guess, she's not talkative right now."

"Who knows? Teenagers!"

"You two having problems?" Jeb asked.

"Actually no, we're having a nice time." I immediately felt a stir, fully understanding that most of the "nice time" was happening because of Robert.

"Can't wait till you can get here, Jeb. There are some interesting things I want you to see. You won't believe it, but I don't want to take up phone time telling you about it."

With a giggle in his voice, "Okay, hon. I'll try to get things settled. Give me a few weeks. I'll be there. I promise."

"A few weeks? In a few weeks, I'll be back to bring Lisa to the airport."

A pause. "Okay. I'll see you when you come home to take Lisa to the airport, and when she returns, I'll bring her back and stay for a week or so. How's that?"

That afternoon, we took a walk in the woods along the side of our cabin. It was cooler there, even with the air thick with humidity.

A fox crossed our path, stopping to watch us, the human invaders. In an instant, the red fox took off, her bushy tail swaying behind her.

Allyson stopped to watch, afraid to move.

"I think it's the mother fox," I whispered.

"I wonder if her babies made it home."

*****

I turned our hamburgers on the outdoor grill as the sun slipped behind the pine trees leaving a pink glow on the perimeter of the sky as a memory of a beautiful day. Two deer stood silently on our shore drinking lake water. I quietly slipped into the cabin to call the girls. The three of us watched from the cabin window until the deer took off into the woods, their white tails pointing toward the colorful sky. Yes, there was beauty in the North.

What a peaceful place to be, I thought. I really wondered why Jeb thought it was so dreadful here.

When the kids retired that night, they were happily anticipating the next day. In fact, Wednesday was marred only by a disturbing message that I found after the girls were asleep. It was another one I wouldn't be sharing with Lisa.

I was brushing my hair in front of the dresser mirror—the one on that awesome honey maple piece that I fell in love with that first day. In fact, I didn't know what possessed me to move the dresser and glance behind the mirror. Maybe it was because we had been finding things behind mirrors and pictures. I thought I had looked behind this particular mirror before during one of our searches, so I surprised myself looking again and actually finding something. The note was written in pencil, and I needed a flashlight to see it clearly.

> We drov thro gh National Forest.
> It was o beautiful in the snow. We sto ped
> by frozen pond in Thunder Pass
> we built a snowman.
> Then Billy took me to his cabin. You cou d
> see for miles from his cabin.

He built a fire in the fire place. We made love there. I could have lost myself there, but then I would never get back. B ck to what not a paradise. O.B. Dec. 1 51

As quiet as I could be, I inched the dresser back in place. Olivia was one confusing woman. Was she telling me that exciting things were in store for me, go for them? Or was she warning me? We're just water skiing, that's all. Besides, the girls are always with me. Oh, and this is a paradise, girl. I wondered just when I took the messages to be written to me personally.

CHAPTER 13

Thursday turned out great! I had all but forgotten the feeling of skimming along the water on a pair of skis. Lisa made it around the lake on her second try and pride salted with thrill shown in her eyes. Allyson preferred to sit in the boat and watch. Robert couldn't talk her into trying the child-sized skis he had thoughtfully brought along.

Later that afternoon, wet towels and swimsuits hung to dry; we all settled down to watch Robert dig a hole in the sand and fill it with fire wood. He placed his grill across the opening and started a roaring fire underneath. Resembling a witch's cauldron, the heavy black pot of water boiled on the grill and a wicked sizzle pierced the air with each raw fish he threw into the pot.

Beads of perspiration formed on Robert's face as he tended his brew. Beads of desire filled my eyes.

"Now watch," he instructed, "this is the best part."

A crackling hiss vibrated through the forest as hot water and steam erupted from the pot like a geyser nearly putting out the flames below. Robert expertly scooped out the fish with a long-handled ladle and placed the flaked delicacy in a baking dish swimming with melted butter and freshly heated cream. It was the best meal we had ever eaten.

"What did I tell you?" He asked as he helped me clean up after supper. "Wasn't this an awesome treat?"

"I must admit I don't know which I enjoyed more, the fried fish or the boil."

I saw Lisa gazing at us as Robert touched my hand when I started to pick up a dirty dish. I quickly removed my hand from the dish. Can't have the kids noticing anything. Right now, this is a private matter. Robert appeared not to notice. Instead, he turned to face the children.

"Have you ever gone shining?" he called out to them.

Allyson and Lisa were finishing the brownie dessert I had bought. They both looked up.

"What's shining?" Lisa asked. "Is it something scary like that movie?"

"Scary?" Robert displayed fake astonishment in his voice. "Not scary, exciting. We'll go tonight as soon as it's dark enough."

*****

Cruising slowly around Butternut Lake, we watched the sky slip into night. An eagle swooped from the shadows above us and pulled a small fish from the watery depths, holding the dangling silver body in his beak as he flew out of sight. A family of ducks swam by toward their shoreline nest. The cry of a loon filled the evening summer air with nature's song. Robert pointed to the black head of the loon sticking out of the water then disappearing again as he dove for his fish meal. When a sprinkling of stars and the small crest of pale white moon hung in the night sky, he stopped the motor and cut the lights. The night engulfed us like a warm dark blanket. Robert stood near the side of the boat and clicked on a bright police search light. Its beam went down into the depths of the murky water, and the lake immediately turned transparent in the light. It was like peering into a gloomy huge fishbowl with gigantic fish, oblivious to the audience watching above them.

"Wow!" Lisa exclaimed, looking over the side. "Look at the size of that fish."

Allyson and I peered over the side of the boat and watched in amazement as Robert turned the light off surrounding us in darkness then quickly back on again making the depths of Butternut Lake a showplace of an assortment of fish swimming under our boat.

I was cognizant not only of the nature show but also of the guy standing next to me. His shoulder brushed mine from time to time. It was uncertain if the contact was on purpose or accidental.

He's good. I thought. He's very sensuous and discreet. But I saw Lisa watching. I better be careful. I wouldn't want to give Lisa any ideas or concerns. And I'm not going to jeopardize my marriage. I love Jeb. At least, I think I do. The uncertainty of my feelings both surprised and frightened me.

*****

Later that night, after Robert left, Lisa appeared in my bedroom as I was sitting in bed writing Jeb a letter. She handed me an envelope addressed to her dad. I was a little concerned about what it contained.

"Add this to the mail."

"I'm writing your dad also," I volunteered.

How could I ask Lisa what she said in her letter without sounding too inquisitive?

"Did you tell your dad about the water-skiing?" I inquired.

Lisa sat down on my bed. "I did. But I didn't tell him who took us. I just said we met a friend."

I tried not to show relief but I felt it.

"I'll be going to Paris in just two weeks." Lisa continued.

"*Deux seamen*," I added remembering to use my French.

I put my pen and pad of paper aside. Obviously, Lisa wanted to talk.

"I know. Are you excited?"

She nodded.

"Will you and Allyson do things with Robert when I'm gone?"

There it was: *the question.*

She's perceptive and worried. Put her at ease. I thought. I reached out and grabbed Lisa's hand.

"I don't think we will. As a matter of fact, Allyson and I might stay home in Milwaukee for a week or so. Sort of check up on your father and have a little break from all the relaxation of the

Northwoods. Then again, your father said he might free himself to come here for a few days when you return. I'll introduce him to Robert, and maybe all of us could do something together."

Lisa seemed to breathe a sigh of relief. "I'm glad. I was hoping you still loved Dad."

I hugged my stepdaughter who seemed so vulnerable and sad.

"Oh, Lisa, of course, I love your dad. After all, you come with him, and I wouldn't want to leave you. Whatever made you think otherwise?" Oops, wrong question. Too late.

She shrugged her narrow shoulders.

"I don't know. Just wanted to be sure, I guess."

"Well, be sure." I answered somewhat relived. "Robert has made this time fun for us, but he isn't your dad. Don't get any funny ideas."

Wow, I thought. *Have I been that transparent?* I better watch myself around teenage eyes. I don't want Lisa to get any wrong ideas. Or were they right ideas? I vowed to myself to stay away from Robert.

Lisa smiled and squeezed my hand.

"I knew it. I was just concerned because I saw him look at you and—"

"And nothing, sweetheart. I'm a diversion to him; he's a diversion to me, and we're just good friends.

I wasn't all that sure anymore. When I closed my eyes at night, I saw Robert. It was Robert I missed during the day. I felt confused and guilty but knew better than to convey any of that to Lisa, especially before her much awaited trip. I put my arms around my stepdaughter who mumbled against my chest.

"I was so worried about you and Robert. That happened with my mom. And then she and dad started fighting. And then—"

The statement was not finished.

Talk about a guilt trip! Oh well, so far, it's just a bunch of feelings. I speculated.

"I won't leave your father. I have no feelings for Robert other than friendship," I lied, hoping it was the truth. "And your dad will be here pretty soon, and all will be well."

I was not as sure as I tried to sound. And that night, I went to bed with a heavy heart and a twitching conscience.

CHAPTER 14

I sipped my morning coffee looking out the window at the lake which effectively mirrored the light grayness of the sky. A sweet smell of rain hung in the early morning air as a small fishing boat whizzed past spraying odors of motor oil. I sighed and held my warm coffee mug as I roamed around the kitchen and living area returning to some of those mysterious Olivia messages, just to make sure they were still there. As I reread each one, I tried to piece together my mother-in-law's life at the cabin. Olivia seemed to have had rare moments of happiness, although most of those moments were a bit illicit and were accompanied by pangs of guilt. Her private thoughts, at times, seemed to mirror my own, and I wondered what our relationship would have been like had I known her. In much of her writing, she sounded lonely, confused, and miserable. I wasn't lonely, confused, or miserable, maybe confused but just a little. I did relate to her attraction to another man and the feelings of guilt that it produced. I wondered if Olivia's recording of her emotions helped her to think more clearly, or was the recording of them supposed to alleviate her guilt. I was sure that Olivia never thought anyone would be able to find the record of her deepest thoughts. Lisa, being a superstitious teenager, viewed some of them as warnings from beyond the grave. I wasn't too sure anymore as to how I viewed them. In some ways, Olivia seemed to think like me and appeared to be speaking directly to me. Spooky.

I refilled my coffee mug letting the steam wash my face. I stood for a moment running my finger along the dim pencil lines of a wall message. I always had been realistic, but lately I didn't trust myself. I shivered at the thought and pushed it from my mind, taking my mug back to the window facing the lake. Gazing at the gray sky made me think that it might be a good day to finish that painting. The kitchen area shone so sunny with the pale yellow paint job I did a couple of weeks ago. It even looked fine with the old wallpaper that I decided not to change because I didn't know how many messages were behind it, and I didn't want to destroy any of that. Fourth of July was a few days away, and within weeks after the holiday, I would be taking Lisa to the airport in Milwaukee. I hoped to have the bedrooms painted before leaving, get rid of that dirty white-gray. It was a sound plan and one to make me stop thinking about things over which I felt scant control like Olivia and Robert.

The day did turn out to be cloudy and cool just as the morning suggested. Wanting to face the hardware store proprietor alone, I dropped the kids off at the park at the tip of the peninsula. On the east side, it had rugged borders, and one could look down at the waves of the lake breaking on rocks. There was a rough-hewed wooden fence along the length of the border to keep onlookers from falling over the edge. Unfortunately, it didn't stop children, and every season, there were a few accidents and at least one death. I had overheard the horror stories in shops, and Robert had spoken of it once. Signs were posted warning parents to watch their little ones. I remember warning the kids to stay away from the east side of the park. The west side was level with the water and boasted a sandy beach, but today was not a day for swimming. It didn't matter because the interior of the park was well-equipped with play equipment, and several families were out enjoying the summer coolness. In fact, the crisp air was almost a relief from what had been a hot and humid start to the summer season. It was the type of cloudy cool day that produced no wetness, and none was predicted. I remember passing interesting shop after interesting shop and making a mental note to stop at one or two on our way back if the stop for paint wouldn't take too much of my time, and there was no reason to assume it would.

The hardware store proprietor was his usual self.

"Back for more paint?" he asked as I walked through his door with the tingling bell.

"Yes, a gallon of blue paint."

He handed me the cards of blues and asked, "What are you painting this time?"

I ignored him and gazed down the color samples until I found the shade I wanted: a dull gray-blue.

"Oh, just the bedrooms," I finally answered.

He busied himself mixing the paint, grabbing brushes, and bagging supplies.

"You find anything strange in that cabin?" he asked.

He startled me. "Strange, like what?"

Ringing up the total and handing me the package, he added, "You know, that Beinfield woman was a weird one, and that cabin holds some secrets for sure."

I took the bag from him and not wanting to discuss our findings with this weird little man, I just dismissed him with, "That Beinfield woman, as you call her, has been gone for some time now. I didn't know her. And it's time people around here forget her and move on."

"Don't be too sure," he answered.

"Too sure of what? That people need to forget or that she's gone?"

It sounded as if he said something under his breath like, *She's not as gone as you think,* but then the bell over the door tinkled, signaling another customer, and the little bizarre man dismissed me with a turn of his head and his greeting to the new arrival. People around here seemed to always be saved by the bell.

On my way out, I noticed reflections in the glass window of a man and his customer discussing something over the counter. Were they discussing me? How paranoid I was becoming. His questions made me wonder if other people had entered the cabin and read messages. What had he meant by "that cabin holds secrets for sure?"

I was beginning to understand why Jeb had bad feelings about being here. The people in this town were weird.

I went to pick up the kids, and there was a lot of commotion in the park, near the drop-off. The sheriff's car was there. I slowed down to look while passing and thought I saw Lisa. Fear gripped my heart as I pulled into a parking spot and ran to her. I was relieved to see her grasping Allyson, but both were in tears. People, mostly teen-age girls, were milling about shouting at each other.

"It was her fault," someone yelled pointing to Lisa.

Robert was trying to calm the crowd.

"Robert," I yelled running to him. "What happened?"

He turned in my direction, but his look was anything but friendly, and my heart stopped. He took me aside to explain.

"A girl fell over the edge."

"Oh my god, no."

"Think she'll be okay. She hung onto the rocks. A little banged up is all. She's on her way to the hospital right now, just to make sure."

The screaming around me escalated, and Robert had to go back to calming the group. I turned to see Lisa coming toward me with Allyson in tow.

"I didn't do it, Steph." She sobbed.

"Do what?"

Robert came toward me again.

"Tell me your side of the story again, Lisa," he asked.

Lisa sniffled back a sob and, in a quiet breathless voice, began.

"Allyson was playing with the other kids in the sand over there." She turned and pointed to the middle of the park where the play equipment was located. "And I was just sitting on the bench. Then these older girls came along and told her to get lost. I didn't get a chance to talk to them because Allyson started running away. I guess she didn't see me on the bench. So I took off after her."

Lisa gulped for air and brushed her hair from her face.

"I caught Allyson, and those girls caught up to us and started pushing us around and saying nasty things. Then that one just fell over the edge. I never pushed her. I mean like I wanted to push her but I didn't. I was holding on to Allyson. But she was yelling at me. They all were yelling, and then that one girl just backed up and dis-appeared. We all screamed and ran to look. She was on a ledge, and the other girls helped her back up. She was bleeding a little on her head and leg. And then they all turned to me and yelled I pushed her. But I didn't."

"I believe her story," Robert assured me.

"This gentleman (he pointed to an elderly couple that just walked up next to him) claims to have seen the whole thing. Says Lisa was running after her sister and the group of girls circled her and bullied her. One of the girls pushed at Lisa and then stepped backward and fell over the cliff."

"That's right. That's what happened. Me and the wife saw the whole thing."

The little gray-haired lady next to the gentleman was bobbing her head in agreement.

"I'm calling all the girls in individually for statements," Robert explained. "Then I'll call the alleged victim. I'll need to talk to Lisa again tomorrow morning also."

With that, he walked back to the circle of four or five hysterical girls trying to calm them. The older couple stayed with us for a moment and tried to be reassuring.

"Don't know how all this started, but me and the wife saw the pushing part. Your girl here was holding her sister's hand, and those other girls were screaming at them. Don't know how that girl fell over the edge. Just lost her footing probably. But we'll go in tomorrow and make an official statement."

His wife just kept bobbing her head.

"Thank you," I said. "We do appreciate your stepping up like this."

On our way home, Lisa told me the story again.

"Those girls were bad," Allyson chimed in.

"What kind of things did they yell at you, Lisa?"

"It happened so fast I don't remember. Just nasty words and telling me to take my little sister and go back to wherever I came from."

"What started it? I mean what lead up to, first of all, the girls chasing Allyson out of the sandbox?"

I drove out of the park almost not stopping at the stop sign, eager to put distance between us and the incident.

"I don't know. I was sitting on the bench listening to my music, and when I looked, those girls were yelling at Allyson. I didn't have time to say anything to them because Allyson started running away, and I chased her."

"It's okay, honey. I have to bring you in to talk to Robert tomorrow morning. Just tell him what you told me. Tell him the whole thing again. That nice older couple is backing up your story."

I wanted an excuse to see Robert, but this was definitely not how I wanted it to go.

We intermittently talked about the incident on the way back to the cabin.

"Did you say anything to those girls either before all this happened or while it was happening?"

"I said nothing. I was listening to my music. It happened so fast, and I was so surprised it was happening at all."

Robert might ask some of these same questions tomorrow. Just remember that older couple is backing up your story.

Thank God the girl survived with minor injuries, and Lisa's statement held, but the incident did something to her. She became quiet and subdued and looked even more forward to leaving for her trip to Paris. I couldn't blame her. As for me, I just became more confused. This northern town was odd. For some strange reason, the town seemed to be against us, my whole family. I asked Robert if those girls had anything to do with the boys (who tried breaking into our cabin that first night). He just said no and left it at that. I asked him what on earth could have caused this commotion. He was very noncommittal and just said that he believed Lisa, and the witnesses bore her out, so let's just call it an unfortunate incident. None of those girls have been in trouble before so who knows what gets in the mind of teenagers these days? I was not satisfied with his answers, and I viewed it more than just an unfortunate incident, but I didn't know what else to do. It was certainly strange.

CHAPTER 15

Fourth of July dawned warm and sunny with just a hint of possible moisture in the air. I had one bedroom painted: mine—looked good.

On our last grocery shopping trip, Lisa had read the posters of Hemlock Bay's Fourth of July celebration, but she was not interested in going after what had happened in the park a few days before. I felt disappointed that Robert hadn't mentioned any plans, but then he probably had to work the day, being the "law enforcement" and all. Jeb couldn't seem to get away for the holiday either. He sent a letter wishing us a happy fourth and said he would be working most of the day. I talked Lisa into just going to the parade, having a hot dog in the park, and calling it a day.

"Just for Allyson."

There would be tons of other people there, and what the heck, you can't let four or five girls scare you away from having a little fun. I must have been convincing.

We dressed in red, white, and blue. Allyson and her doll, Mary Jane, had blue and red stars painted on their fat little cheeks, thanks to Lisa. We were patriotic and ready. Allyson was beaming in excitement all the way to town. She didn't seem to have a problem going back to the park. Kids forget things quickly. Hemlock Bay had outdone itself with flags on every pole along the street, colorful bunting hanging from all the shop windows, and streamers of red and blue attached building to building across the street. Masses of people were already lining the curb waiting for the parade. I wondered where all these people came from, crawling out of the woods like ants to a picnic. What a contrast with our first trip into town! So much had happened since then! Faint sounds of parade bands practicing somewhere wafted through the car windows. It was hard not to get caught up in the celebratory mood. Lisa passed her time plugged into her music while surveying the streets looking for her torturers. Poor girl.

I did notice Robert's car parked in the station parking lot, and I hate to admit it, but my heart gave a leap, but he was nowhere in sight. It was probably good. I did secretly hope we'd run into each other. Our interview after "the incident" had been stiff and formal, and it left me with a sour taste.

Parking was not allowed along the streets today and the area in front of the bakery and the post office was filled. The parade was assembling in the parking lot of Ed's Grocery store at the beginning of town. Even the two churches, one Protestant and the other Catholic, had filled parking yards. We found what had to be one of the last remaining places to park. Once out of the car, we experienced the challenge of weaving sideways through the sea of humanity, so Allyson would be able to see. "Excuse me" seemed to be the phrase of the day.

"Isn't that the Beinfield woman and her kids?"

It was almost a whisper. When I turned, no one seemed to be looking my way, so we just continued to the curb. I hated the way I was starting to get obsessed.

After the parade, we moved like a glued group into the park. Children skipped along the paths and played tag around the trees. Groups of teenagers idly talked and laughed holding red paper cups of cokes. The girls we dreaded were nowhere to be seen, and that was good. I know Lisa was watching. What a terrible predicament for her! I was happy she had a trip coming up. There were stands selling all sorts of goodies and tables of trinkets. The air was filled with excitement and sweet smells. I was filled with loneliness in a sea of partygoers. There was a strange feeling I was beginning to have every time I came to town. I felt as if I were being followed or at least watched. I would turn quickly to see no one. Once or twice, I saw a shadow of something, like a ghost it would be there, then quickly disintegrate into thin air. The creepy vision wasn't visible long enough to make out a man or woman. I imagined my mind was playing tricks on me.

I noticed it today in the crowd. I'd feel the stare; I'd turn to look. It was there and then it wasn't.

By noon, we were sticky and full feasting on hot dogs, ice cream cones, and cinnamon buns. Allyson had a blotch of ketchup from her half eaten hot dog dribbling down her blue T-shirt. Damp odor of impending rain floated in the air as we headed back to the cabin.

The strangest thing happened that night. We watched the fireworks from around the lake sitting on our pier. Rain was predicted, but the sky stayed clear for the fireworks. The kids had pop, and I poured myself a few vinos. Allyson fell asleep in my lap, and Lisa complained of being tired and turned in early also. I washed our few dishes and sat on the wicker couch with another wine just gazing out the window. It had been a warm and humid day, and the evening air felt refreshing. A slight steamy fog had just begun to rise from the lake—the precursor before the predicted showers. I'm sure the vacationers were happy the firework display was earlier. I could see patches of the moon slip in and out of cloud cover. As I gazed out the window sipping on my wine, the cabin quiet with my sleeping brood, I thought I could make out an outline at the end of the pier which seemed more defined in the patches of moonlight. I really didn't think anyone was out there, but every so often, I did catch a glimpse. The form I was trying to make out disappeared when the sky was dark, but when the moon sliced through a cloud, a definite shape took place. It appeared to be female mainly because of a white flimsy wrap of some sort. I opened the window.

"Hey," I called out. "Who's there?"

The figure turned and looked at the cabin, real spooky-like. I felt a little easier thinking it was a female character, and I could just made out short dark hair framing her face with short bangs across her forehead, but face features were indistinguishable.

"Hey," I called out again. "Who are you?"

The moon slipped back into its cloud cover, and the appearance looked like a blob of fog again. My heart was in my throat, but I was curious. I put down my wine glass and went to the door, turning on the bright porch light before going out. The mistiness added a wet wool smell to the air, yet it wasn't thick enough to hamper visibility totally. The porch light shed a watery glow as far as the pier. I saw her, then I didn't. She seemed to turn and stare at me when I yelled, but I couldn't make out her face, just the hair style. And she never moved away or made any sound. As I neared the spot, goosebumps of fear claimed me, and I felt foolish. She appeared to disappear in thin air as I walked out on the pier. No one was there! She could not have left without passing me or jumping in the water. But she was gone. And she sure had looked more solid than just imagination.

"Is anyone out here?" I turned in a circle, demanding of the silence.

The dismal water sloshed the shore, but I stood alone. Feeling ridiculous, I turned back toward the cabin. The haze permeated the air like a thick blanket, and there in the porch light, I thought I saw her again! It was the white robe and the short bob hair with the straight bangs framing a featureless face. I quickened my step and yelled. "Hey, stay there. Who are you?"

How did she get there from the pier without passing me?

Silence greeted me. As I got closer, she seemed to be retreating. By the time I reached the porch, I could hardly make her out. She seemed to be half way down my drive, moving without actually moving at all.

"Hey," I called again.

But the object (or person) dissolved into fog. I was not going to chase a ghost down the drive! A ghost! Now I was losing it!

Back inside the cabin, door closed and locked, I rested my head against the wood frame to calm down. Obviously, if she was a real person, she didn't want to be known. I doubted the real person part, feeling like an idiot for my doubt. My first impulse was to call Robert. But then what would I tell him? I thought I saw a figure in the fog in a flowing white robe, and she dissolved into thin air? He'd think I was crazy. I was beginning to think I was crazy. Nothing was destroyed or broken into. She could have entered the cabin. She didn't. I double checked the locked door, retrieved my wine glass, and poured out the remainder of the contents in the sink. My empty wine bottle sat on the table. *Too much wine*, I thought, *I think I'm seeing ghosts.*

CHAPTER 16

It stormed all night and into the following day. And I mean stormed! Sheets of rain, lightening blasts that tore the sky in half, roaring thunder, just like the day we drove up here. In the middle of the night, I had a guest in my bedroom: Allyson. During the next day, Lisa and I took turns quieting her after each blast of thunder. The lights flickered and then went out. It was daylight without any power, and we had a cake in the oven! The baking project was one way to entertain and quiet Allyson. I was glad for the gas stove. At least we wouldn't end up with chocolate mush instead of our cake. Around noon, the sky quieted, but the downpour continued. By two o'clock, the lights flickered and came on again. The three of us sat around the small living area absorbed in books or puzzles. It was too nasty outside for even a trip to town. It turned out to be the perfect day to follow a somewhat haunted evening—the stuff stories are about. One day, I might write a book about all of this. I tried to forget about the vision I thought I saw last night. But that didn't mean it stopped bothering me. To be honest, I was freaked out. After all those times I thought I was seeing a shadow or a ghost that kept disappearing, last night the image stayed. I mean, it (or she) didn't stay for long but at least I could make something out. This was becoming way too disturbing. I wish I had another adult to share the information with. I just didn't want to scare Lisa, and I didn't care to share this with Robert because I didn't want him to think I was delusional. I really didn't know where to go with this. So I just kept it to myself.

"Hey, Steph," Lisa interrupted my thoughts, "what's that square door thingy in the ceiling between the bedroom doors?"

I shifted in my seat to get a better look.

"Oh, that. Think it's an attic."

"So what do you think is up there?"

"Beats me." I went back to my book.

"How do you get in with a door in the ceiling?" Lisa persisted.

"You probably pull it open, and there's a folded ladder of some sort. We had one in our house when I was a kid. Called it a disappearing stairway."

Lisa got up from her seat to stand under it. Then she pulled a kitchen chair over to reach a small piece of rope tied to the door.

"I didn't notice the ceiling door before."

"That's because it's made of tongue and groove wood pieces like the rest of the ceiling," I answered as she tugged at the rope.

At first, her pulls produced no results, but as she kept tugging, the square gave way with a squeak, and the small door opened slowly.

"You're right. There's a ladder folded up in here."

I put down my book, and both Allyson and I went to stand under the door.

"What do you think is up there?" Lisa asked.

"Don't know. Let's have a look."

I helped her tug on the ladder which unfolded and almost touched the floor.

I told Allyson to stay down, then I climbed up with Lisa close behind.

"Get the flashlight, it's dark up here."

Allyson ran to get the flashlight for us and handed it to Lisa who handed it to me. Not only was it dark but hot and stuffy—a real sauna. The rain pinged on the roof with an eerie rhythm as the flashlight beam cut through the darkness. I made sure there was a solid floor before I climbed inside followed by Lisa. We crawled along slowly. It's a bit of a disorientated feeling climbing into an attic especially if the roof isn't high enough for a person to stand up. The flashlight illuminated some old curtain rods in the corner and two chairs laying on their sides. There were three cardboard boxes of differing sizes. And a small chest like a hope chest or a cedar chest. We crawled over to the boxes. One was actually empty. The other two seemed to contain old curtains and blankets. Sweat was dripping down my back, and I knew I couldn't be up there for too much longer; the air was stifling.

"Let's see if any of this stuff is worthwhile. If not, we can dump it." I slid two boxes to the opening, and Lisa grabbed one end as she descended the ladder. Next came the chest. We hadn't opened it. Even if it was empty, I thought we might be able to use it for something. It appeared in rather good condition. It was a bit tricky getting it down the ladder.

By the time we folded the ladder and closed the opening, we were hot, dusty, sweaty, and exhausted. We rummaged through the boxes first. Nothing but old ugly curtains and only one blanket worth keeping. We threw everything back in the boxes for our trip to the dump. Next came the chest.

"A treasure chest, a treasure chest." Allyson squealed.

At first, we thought it might be locked. After a little tugging, we pried the top open to an explosion of dust. Coughing and waving at the dust particles in the air, we peered inside. It contained some clothes wrapped in tissue. We unwrapped a rather large maroon wool sweater and an old navy winter jacket. Carefully pulling a parcel from the bottom, we laid it on the floor and proceeded to unwrap the crunchy yellowed tissue. Inside its ripping folds was a silky fabric—a very light pink silk bathrobe. My heart stopped. I held it up, and a pang of recognition hit me. My ghost! The lady I saw last night. Her white gown could have been this light pink robe! It had to be a coincidence.

"Steph, what's wrong? You look like you just saw a ghost!"

"Um, well—"

"I smell something burning!" Lisa jumped up and ran to the oven.

I was saved by a chocolate cake. It came out looking like, well, something like a cake.

"If we cover it with frosting, it might not be too bad," I offered.

We left the "cake" to cool and returned to our investigating work. As I refolded the robe and rewrapped it, Lisa discovered a box of old photos in the corner of the chest and started sorting through them. I placed the robe package back inside the chest. The kids hadn't asked anything about it, and I hadn't told them about my vision last night and decided I wasn't going to. It made no sense to frighten them. I swallowed a sour lump in my throat just fingering the soft fragile fabric of the robe, like I was touching something dead. I'm sure this was all just a stupid coincidence. Allyson lost interest in the chest and went back to her coloring book. There were no treasures as far as she was concerned. Lisa ruffled through the old photos.

"Let me see some of those."

She handed me the pictures she had gone through; they were mostly pictures of someone's catch of fish and several of the cabin being built in various stages of completion. The pictures were small squares and all glossy black and white, most with white scalloped edges. Then I came across the picture that made my heart stop. It was a couple in front of the unfinished cabin. The picture was clear, but the couple wasn't close enough to really see features. The man was in long dark pants and short sleeve light shirt. The woman had on a flowered dress of some sort down to her knees. But it was her hair that popped out at me—short, dark with even bangs across the forehead.

"Lisa, is this your grandma and grandpa?"

She peered over at the photo.

"Doesn't look like grandma. And I never met grandpa."

"Well, don't forget, this couple is young, like before your dad was even born."

"Hmm," she mused and then went back to the pile of photos she held in her hand.

I turned the picture over. In slanted small-lettered handwriting similar to the handwriting on our hidden messages, it simply said, *Les and me.*

CHAPTER 17

"I found one!" Lisa called excitedly from her bedroom.

"You found the T-shirt, that's good," I answered absentmindedly, referring to the T-shirt Lisa had been looking for to complete her packing.

"I found my shirt a while ago," Lisa answered as I poked my head into the children's bedroom.

"I meant I found a message! And it's really a strange one, Steph. Come and look."

"I thought you were packing, Lisa."

I walked into the room. Allyson was sitting on the bed absorbed with her dolls.

"What are you doing with the dresser away from the wall?"

"I dropped a bracelet and had to move the dresser to find it. Then I found this.

And you know what, Steph, I did look behind here before, and there was nothing there at the time. It's weird."

We got on our knees to get a better view of the message scribbled in pencil behind the dresser. Allyson came to join us, squeezing in between. I put my arm around my younger child and leaned close to Lisa to read the message. It was clearly readable without missing letters. Thank God. But it was so disturbing.

He was born. Jeffery Edward. Minnow Point Memorial.

I thought Les would be thrilled. He's so distant.

I thought we'd go home. But we came back here.

I'm so afraid of the pantry.

Les built kitchen cupboards—a surprise.

But I'll make him get rid of the pantry.

Olivia, June '58

"Didn't I tell you it's a strange message? Do you get it? It's about my dad. And it's so weird that I didn't see it before," Lisa repeated.

I read it again. It was about Jeb's birth all right. He apparently was born up here, and Les didn't seem too thrilled at his birth. Wonder why? Maybe that was part of Jeb's dread of this place. A gnawing pain grabbed the pit of my stomach. I was glad to be leaving for a while. Disturbing messages, an actual "real life" ghost haunting the pier a few days ago—it was a bit much. I couldn't come to grips with that image I saw, and I was trying to forget it, blaming it on too much wine. But every so often, the girl at the end of the pier came back to disturb me. And now I had a lost pantry to worry about. Geez, time to get in the car and leave.

"What pantry is she talking about? Where is it? And why is she scared of it?" Lisa was full of questions.

I rose to my feet and quietly replaced the dresser.

"I don't know. The cabin doesn't have a pantry, at least not one we can locate. I'm finding your grandmother to be a rather complex woman."

Then in an effort to be more cheerful I said, "We're on a time schedule. You have a plane to Paris to catch, remember? Let's finish packing."

Where had the summer gone? I couldn't believe that we had been at the cabin for six weeks already.

I walked over to Lisa's suitcase on the bed and, in a true mother fashion, began to rearrange things for a better fit. I just didn't want to deal with Olivia at the moment. Lisa brought more things that I helped her to arrange, but we were both absorbed in thought.

"If you find more messages while I'm gone, will you remember where they are and show them to me when I get back?"

"Of course." I helped her close the suitcase, feeling a pang of guilt at the messages I had found and not shared. There are some things a young girl doesn't need to know.

"Will you bring back a present for me?" Allyson asked.

"I'll find something *especially* nice for Ellie." Lisa gave her a bear hug.

*****

Do I ever remember the day! I woke that morning with a foreboding feeling I couldn't place but contributed it to the misery of the long drive ahead. We left after a quick lunch. The day was hot and still. The air felt heavy.

"What a strange color everything is," I remarked to no one in particular as we climbed into the car. A dull peach salmon sky cast the feel of sunset rather than noon. Lisa and Allyson did not seem to be aware of anything, caught up as they were—one in the excitement of her impending trip, the other with the thought of losing her big sister. The two girls sat in back, Allyson clinging to Lisa like glue, sharing her Mary Jane doll and coloring books. Lisa being a terrific big sister played along with her.

Bags of corn curls, chips, and pretzels as well as a cooler of soda were packed to sustain us on our five-hour trip to the airport. Nicole and her parents would be waiting for us there. And hopefully, Jeb could take some time off to be there for the great farewell. He hadn't promised, but his last letter indicated that he sure would try. He also promised that he would try to return north for a few days with Allyson and me.

I half thought that possibly Robert might stop over to say goodbye. He didn't. And why should he? We were nothing but friends, and he was probably busy.

"Gosh, look at that sky." I peered through the windshield at the wisps of steel gray clouds building up on the perimeter of the horizon as we turned onto the highway. I couldn't ever remember seeing a sky like it. Feeling a pang of concern, I stopped my tape and turned on the local radio station. The music was interrupted with a weather bulletin predicting a possible tornado.

"Great!" I gasped.

Lisa sat up and took notice. "Hey, it really looks weird outside. Do you think we'll get a tornado?"

I tried to hide my concern. "It's for Forest County. We should be out of the county in about twenty minutes. I don't think we'll have to worry about it. Plus, it's only a watch, right now."

"What's a watch?" She asked.

"It means conditions are ripe for a tornado to develop, but so far, none have been spotted on the ground. If a funnel cloud is spotted, the watch turns into a warning. Then we worry about it."

I pushed the accelerator a bit faster than normal. I would feel better once we left Forest County.

"I don't like tomatoes. They're scary," Allyson piped up from the back. "I saw one once on the *Wizard of Oz.*"

"It's a tor-na-do, not a tomato." Lisa laughed. "And I'm older than you, and I never saw one. So don't worry about it."

How well Lisa plays the big sister role. I mused. I'm really going to miss her these next two weeks.

Lisa was back to questioning me. "If it turns into a warning, what would we do?"

Hmmm, that was a good one. What would we do?

Before I could come up with an answer, there was another bulletin.

"Sh," I said. "Listen."

Just our luck, the watch became a warning, just like that. And the area covered was extended to include the counties we needed to travel through.

"Shit," I said a bit too loud. We were traveling south, passing right through Mitchell and Fond du Lac Counties.

"Mommy, you said a bad word," my three-year-old conscience from the back.

"Mommy's sorry. I'll be more careful. Guess the weather is adding to the excitement of the day. Let's hope for the best. I'm sure we'll be fine," I said with more confidence than I felt.

"Will my plane take off?" Lisa asked.

"I'm sure it will, they didn't say anything about Milwaukee."

"Well, what would we do if we saw a tornado?" Lisa persisted.

I wasn't sure; my memory bank hadn't any precautions listed. I tried to think of things I might have heard.

"We could drive parallel to it or try to outrun it. If all else fails, we could find a ditch and lie in it to protect ourselves against flying debris, I guess."

"My mommy's smart about tomatoes cause she's a teacher." Allyson sounded more confident than I felt.

Lisa turned to her. "Tor-na-do, silly. Say it right."

*****

An hour of stressful driving and I found myself at the southern end of Mitchell County gazing at a tangerine sky with angry dark clouds forming around the perimeter. And it didn't help that the radio kept blaring to take cover.

How can anything so potentially deadly be so beautiful? I wondered.

The sky was becoming increasingly darker, and vehicles were filling the off-ramps and leaving the freeway. I spotted a fast-food restaurant just beyond the next off-ramp. *Might be a good idea to pull off and get something to eat and wait out this storm.* Tornadoes usually travel west to east. This potential one looks like it might be south of us—our driving direction! We need to stop, possibly wait it out. I wondered if restaurants have tornado shelters. I took a chance. Gazing at the dashboard clock, it was a little after two. Lisa's plane was scheduled to leave at nine. That gave us ample time for a stop. We turned on the off-ramp.

"Where are we going?" Lisa inquired.

"Thought we'd stop and wait out the storm. We could order some cokes and fries. And maybe use the restroom?"

Restroom, I thought, *no windows*. I remember hearing something about seeking an inside room without windows for a tornado shelter. Worth a try.

The yellow arches paled against the bright orange sky. As we entered, the uniformed workers were filing out.

"Hey lady, we're leaving." A young man with greasy hair passed by. "There's a storm coming."

"The radio says the storm is southwest of here. I think we'll be all right." I held onto the door trying to convince myself as well as the departing help.

"Just the same, we're out of here." The young man called back as he ran to his car. "Help yourself. It's free."

I had no idea where they thought they were going. Maybe home to a basement safe room? I hoped they were wrong, and the storm would pass us by.

"This is kind of creepy," Lisa whispered as we entered the empty restaurant bathed in the hazy citrus light.

"Mommy, can we take all the fries we want?" Allyson was eager to start helping herself to the goodies, but I ushered them into the restroom first.

"If the storm starts before we leave, we can come in here. We should be safe." I sounded more confident than I felt. Actually, fear curled like a knot inside of me. But Lisa and Allyson were excited about helping themselves to free food.

"Wow, this is sure cool!" Miss "Watch-Her-Weight" was behind the counter filling bags with fries, and it was difficult to see if more was getting in the bags or into her mouth.

Allyson was close behind, joining in the fun.

"Hey girls, let's not be piggies." I was not too sure of the moment's activity.

No one else was in the building.

"But, Steph, all this stuff will be wasted if we don't take it. They can't sell this stuff an hour from now."

How true—the wisdom of a fifteen-year-old.

"This is cool, really cool."

"Really cool," Allyson echoed as she followed behind Lisa filling her bag and her mouth with gusto.

I stood guard at the window, watching the southwestern sky. If I saw a funnel, heaven forbid, we'd head for the restroom. I noticed the parked cars starting up and heading, some back down the freeway, others off the ramp to the side street. What did they know that we didn't?

Oh well, when will there be another day as strange as this one? I shrugged my shoulders and started filling a bag with wrapped burgers that were sitting under an amber warming light that was turned off, of course. But my eyes and ears were never far from the windows. The darkened western sky although more intense seemed to have receded making it seem like we may not be in the path of the storm after all. The southern sky started to look less ominous, and I assumed the cars were getting back on the road in an effort to outrun the tornado in case it decided to change directions again. The strangest thing was the stillness. Not a breeze. My head felt stuck in a void.

"Girls!" I yelled back into the store. "Grab your stuff and let's go. *Now!*"

Conscience grabbing hold, I dug into my pocket and threw some dollar bills on the counter. *Stupid thing to do if this place is blown away*, I thought.

"They said it was free, Steph," Lisa complained as I grabbed my bags in my left hand and held onto Allyson's arm with my right.

"Never mind. Just hurry."

I figured if all the other cars were getting on the road and going somewhere, they knew something I didn't know. I'd follow suit.

Lisa and Allyson were busy munching as I pulled the car back on the freeway. A glance in the car's side mirror was shocking, indicating a change in storm direction again. The sky was now jet black.

"Look where we just came from!" Lisa yelled. "It looks like midnight."

No sooner were we on the road when cars started pulling off to the side again. People were getting out and running. In the rearview mirror, I spotted an ominous cloud of dark dust descending from the blackened sky. My heart skipped a beat or maybe two or three. *Think fast*, I told myself. Something I really had trouble doing, think fast. What should we do?

Up ahead was a cement embankment—a bridge over the freeway. People seemed to be running toward it for shelter. I drove as close as I could to eliminate running distance and slipped my car almost sideways into a spot between two other cars on the side of the road.

"Everybody get out," I commanded. "We're going to run toward that bridge like everybody else is doing."

Allyson dropped her doll in the road but held fast to her bag of fries as she scrambled out of the car. I picked her up.

"My Mary Jane, my Mary Jane." She yelled, her small arm waving in the air above my shoulder.

But we didn't stop long enough to even close the car doors. The little lost doll lay still in the road. People jumped over it or ran around it as they headed toward the cement embankment. It wasn't windy. It was hot and still—death still. The only sounds were running footsteps, a cry now and then, and blaring car horns. There were so many quiet people under the bridge by the time we got there that I wondered if there would be room for all of us. A funny thought came to mind about not seeking shelter under bridges, but I couldn't remember the reason why not so I just did what everybody else was doing.

"Push the children up the embankment toward the top of the bridge." Someone yelled.

People were lifting and pushing their children up the cement embankment. Some adults were climbing up as well. Climbing and slipping and climbing, that is. Before I could do anything, a powerful gust of wind sounding like a speeding locomotive swirled under the bridge pushing us to the ground. I remembered flinging out my right hand to grab Lisa. A hissing roar deafened our ears. Screams and cries mixed with the roar until one couldn't tell which sounds were from the storm and which came from the population under the bridge. Thumps and bangs were followed by a deadening silence and equally eerie calm. The wails and cries of children started as people were picking themselves up and venturing out to look at the sky.

"It's over," someone said.

"Are you okay, Lisa?"

"I'm okay."

Allyson, who was too stunned to even cry, had a scraped knee but appeared unharmed. I picked her up and stumbled to the road. Everyone was moving as if dumbfounded.

Tree branches and assorted debris were scattered over the highway. Shattered glass crunched underfoot as we made our way back to the car. The cars parked on the freeway appeared to all have gone through a different turmoil—some with broken windows, some laying on their sides, some seemingly untouched. Our vehicle was intact with three doors hanging open as we left it. One small hamburger lay next to the door, trampled by running feet. Our fries were scrambled along the freeway like the bread crumbs in *Hansel and Gretel*. So much for free food. There was a soft murmur of voices and few calls as people located their vehicles. Some engines were starting up. A few horns honked. Children were crying.

"Where's Mary Jane?" Allyson cried as I put her down to get into the car.

Lisa and I looked around the car for the missing doll. It seemed so trifle to be looking for a doll after what we had been through.

"I think Mary Jane might be in Oz," Lisa finally said, and Allyson accepted that after a few sobs, of course.

It's difficult to describe the feelings after one survives a calamity—shaky, exhilarating, heart-thumping. Allyson was whimpering a bit about her doll, but in reality, I knew that her cries were as much from the scare we had just survived.

People with cars running were offering rides to stunned individuals looking at their overturned vehicles. I didn't think another person could fit in our car, crammed as it was with suitcases and snacks, but I did look for one or two people along the highway to offer a ride, but all seemed to be taken care of.

"Wait 'till I tell Nicole about this," Lisa commented as I carefully maneuvered around the debris on the freeway.

The sky to our west was still dark broken with flashes of lightening looking like floodlights being turned off and on in the black abyss. To the east and north, the sky glowed strange mustard yellow. But to the south, which was our destination, it looked a normal misty gray, like any rainy day. The radio blared with news of the damage in Oakfield where the tornado had struck with all its fury.

"Where's Oakfield?" Lisa asked.

"I'm not sure. I think it's a little west of where we were. I think we were on the edge of the tornado, not actually in it," I answered.

"We were in it. I saw it."

Now that she had survived, Lisa didn't want to downplay the adventure.

"I thought I saw it too. But since there is so much damage in Oakfield, I don't think we felt the full force of the storm. Hard to believe, isn't it?"

Police and ambulance sirens were heard in the distance. I swerved a couple of times around assorted trash in the road. Then we entered an area of steady falling rain and gray skies. The windshield wipers swished the drops to the side; the trip back to Milwaukee was eerily similar to our trip north.

"Mommy, will more tomatoes come?" Allyson cried.

"Tor-na-does," Lisa corrected, softer this time.

"Tor-na-toes," Allyson repeated.

"One is enough honey," I answered. "Now it is just going to rain."

By the time we approached Milwaukee, the air had cooled, and a thin mist fell, but my nerves were frayed. I glanced at the clock on the dash—seven o'clock. Five hours had passed since we stopped. I didn't think our stop was that long, and I seemed to be making good time on the freeway, but five hours is five hours! I accelerated, passing several cars, hoping the state patrol wasn't anywhere nearby.

I found a parking place rather close to the front door of the terminal.

Once inside, it was a mad dash to get through the ticket line and to Gate 7. In 1996, visitors were allowed right up to the gate. In retrospect, I don't know how I would have felt later had I left Lisa to maneuver the airport on her own. Nicole was standing worriedly next to her mother. She was at least an inch taller than Lisa with the broad shoulders of a swimmer; her long flowing hair was the color and texture of corn silk from the months of chlorinated pool water.

"*Bonsoir*," the two friends exchanged excitedly in deep hugs.

"Lisa! I was so worried you would be late!"

"It's okay." Lisa's mother waved to me. "The flight's been delayed an hour due to the weather."

Trudy Blancard was the older image of Nicole, being a swimmer in high school herself. Broad shoulders did her justice fitting perfectly into the jacket of her light blue linen suit. Trudy's blond hair was cut short; her rhinestone earrings (maybe diamonds, who knows) were glistening in her ears.

"Speaking of the weather," she said as I got closer, "how was your drive?"

I barely opened my mouth to answer when Lisa cut in.

"You won't believe it!" And Lisa took over the storytelling. Of course, Lisa had us almost up through the funnel swirling with rooftops and trees!

By this time, Mr. Blancard joined us, briefcase in hand since this was a business trip for him. He had been looking impatiently at his watch. A tall and thin man, always in a suit, he pushed at his black-rimmed glasses with his forefinger lifting them back in place. It was a Clark Kent move, although his features were soft and spongy-looking, nothing like the original Superman of TV fame.

"You don't mean to say that you actually drove right through a tornado?"

I winked at Nicole's parents. "I believe we did," I whispered, "but not quite as horrific as Lisa is explaining. The brunt of the storm hit Oakfield according to the radio. But we spent about twenty minutes under a bridge with tons of people. And yes, it was quite an experience. I'm still shaking and nervous."

"I'm glad you're all okay," a male voice broke in behind me.

"Dad, you came." Lisa ran to Jeb's waiting arms.

"Wouldn't miss telling you to stay clear of the Frenchmen."

"Don't worry, Dad," Lisa answered, "I'm going to see the Eiffel Tower."

"Right." I laughed as I watched Jeb pick up Allyson and give her a hug too. I got an arm around me and a peck on the cheek. "Glad to see you, hon."

Jeb's five o'clock shadow scratched my face. Normally, it would have given him a manly, sexy look, but tonight, it just looked bedraggled if not a bit sloppy. His eyes clouded with tiredness, tended to look murkier green than the gorgeous blue they had been before, and his dark hair was a bit longer and messier than usual. I was disappointed in how he looked in contrast to ever tailored Mr. Blancard.

"Hi there, Jeb, glad you could make it." Thomas Blancard extended his hand for shaking.

"Hi, Tom." (Jeb was the only one who refused to call him Thomas.) "Thanks for taking Lisa with you."

"No problem."

We had time for a few other pleasantries before they were called to board.

"*Au Revoir*," Lisa waved and then excitedly disappeared with Nicole's family through the walkway to the waiting plane. The last thing I saw was her bright young face throwing kisses and smiling ear to ear. Jeb, Allyson, and I watched the plane taxi down the runway and lift carelessly into the gray sky. I'm so glad departure wasn't as impersonal as it is today. I think, with the events that followed, I would have been even more upset without a proper goodbye.

CHAPTER 18

"Did you have to park far from here?" Jeb asked as we walked to the front doors.

"Actually no, we're rather close."

It was nice to see Jeb. I realized how much I had missed him. Allyson too was happy to be with her father. She rambled on and on about the tornado, saying it correctly.

We went for a late pizza, hoping Allyson could make it through the meal. And me, too, for that matter. It had been a horrific day.

"So what have you guys been doing up north?"

"We met a nice man and went in his boat," Allyson contributed between bites.

"Oh is that so?" Jeb looked at me with raised eyebrows.

I rushed to fill him in on the almost intruders of the first night and calling the sheriff. Then I explained about the boat ride as if it were a single event, hoping my darling would shut her mouth. I don't know why I felt so guilty. It had been innocent fun. It did seem to satisfy Jeb, thank goodness, except he wanted to know why I hadn't informed him about the intruder.

"Didn't want to worry you," that was my explanation. "since we seemed to have taken care of it."

It wasn't until bedtime that my sweet big mouthed daughter truly missed her doll.

She yawned and, with eyes half closed, asked, "Will my Mary Jane get back from Oz?"

"If she doesn't, mommy will make sure you have a new Mary Jane."

Allyson sobbed a little but was too tired for a complete blowup and drifted off to sleep.

At eleven, Lisa called from New York to announce they had arrived safely. She had found her first plane ride to be enjoyable and was looking forward to seeing some of New York tonight and flying to Paris tomorrow night. You'd think between a tornado and your first plane ride, you'd be exhausted. Not at fifteen, I guess. But I, on the other hand, was, and I went to bed following Lisa's call. My back and head ached from the strain of the day.

Allyson was in the family room watching cartoons the next morning. Guess she had missed the television a bit.

"Good morning, sweetheart."

"Make me pancakes, Mommy. Okay?"

"I'll see what I can do."

Jeb had made coffee and was sitting at the table reading the paper and sipping a cup. He got up to pour one for me. Then handed me my hot coffee with a peck on my cheek. Six weeks away and so far, I scored two pecks on the cheek. (Well, last night was mostly my fault being shaken and exhausted from the drive.)

"Morning, sweetheart. I know we planned that you would stay home a week or two, but I'm so swamped at work; I'll be leaving early and staying late. If you want, why not go back north and enjoy yourself?"

I must admit, I was a bit taken back. I thought he'd be happy we were home (and maybe a little romantic), take a day or two off? I looked at my husband with accusing eyes. Was he seeing someone? He seemed a bit disengaged. At this point, I wasn't sure I cared and that scared me.

"Actually, Jeb, we were planning on spending some time with you. And you did write that you would come back with Allyson and me and stay at the cabin for a week."

"Ah, I did write that, didn't I?"

He got up to pour us both more coffee.

"On the plus side, honey, the business is going gang busters, and if this continues, it'll pay for itself in about a year and a half." He took a thoughtful sip and continued. "I hired more staff a few weeks ago, and they're working out well. By the time Lisa comes back from France, I should be able to leave for a bit. I can bring her back up north and save you another trip. I should be able to stay a few days to a week at that time. How's that?"

How's that? I didn't know how I felt about *that.* For some reason, I was starting not to care. It made my decision of a possible liaison with Robert seem more legit. Jeb seemed to be giving me one excuse after another. Would that make it right? He raised his coffee mug in a toast. Needless to say, I was muffed, but I would never admit it, not even to myself, something was pulling me back to the Northwoods. Was it the peacefulness of the tall pines swaying in the breeze, the sun sparkling off the lake water? Or was the pull Robert? Maybe the tug I felt was more intense, like Olivia and her messages. Then it dawned on me, I never said anything to Jeb or anyone else for that matter about those scribbles we had found. I guess I thought they were only the musing of an overly imaginative teenage daughter and her slightly superstitious stepmother. Anyway, getting back to Robert, it had all been innocent fun, and I pooh-poohed the idea of anything else. Besides, Allyson was with me, and experience showed she would keep me honest. But, as I mentioned before, Jeb had no time for us. I knew he was busy, and I loved him, I think. I wasn't too sure anymore. I needed romance, adventure. And wasn't Olivia trying to tell me that? Oh geez, here I go, believing in ghosts! That became my calling card, my excuse. Right or wrong, it eased my conscience.

CHAPTER 19

It was a lonely ride without Lisa. Not that Lisa had been that much company. She spent most of the trip sleeping or plugged into earphones. But just having an "almost" adult along had made the trip to the cabin more interesting. Allyson colored in her books and slept. We stopped for hamburgers and fries, this time paying for our food but also being able to eat in peace. I bought Allyson a small doll at a gas station shopping mart. It didn't actually replace her Mary Jane, but it was a start.

Arriving at the cabin about four in the afternoon, my heart gave a leap to see Robert's car parked in the drive. He was just rounding the corner of the cabin.

"Hi…hi, Allyson." He waved and came to open the car door for us.

"I was just checking things out. I didn't expect you back so quickly."

"The weather turned sunny; Jeb was super busy with work, and we couldn't stay away." I smiled weakly.

"Speaking of weather, did you manage to stay ahead of that storm the other day?"

"Actually no, we didn't."

He helped carry our bags into the cabin.

"You're kidding. What happened?"

He listened intently as the story was retold, for the hundredth time, I thought. But, somehow, the retelling seemed fresh and exciting this time.

"You did the right thing," he assured me.

"I have a picture for you." Allyson tore a colored picture out of her coloring book and handed it to Robert.

"Hey, this is special. I'm going to hang it in my office and think of you."

Voices blared on his car radio. He hurried to his car and answered pulling the phone through the window.

"I have to run."

Then, as an afterthought as he got in the car, "I'm really glad you both are safe—and back."

I felt a pang of disappointment watching him leave, realizing how lonely it was going to be with evening coming.

As he started to pull out, he hung his head out the open window.

"I'd like to take you and Allyson out for dinner. Would it be all right if I came back in about two hours?"

I was caught a bit off guard. "I-I don't know."

"We won't stay late, and I think you will like the place I have in mind."

"Well—"

A zillion thoughts played in my head like practically promising Lisa we wouldn't be seeing Robert. I dismissed the thoughts. After all, he did say me and Allyson. What could possibly happen with Allyson along?

"Well, all right. We'll go."

"Great, see you about six-thirty."

I climbed the three wooden cabin steps as he pulled away. Entering the kitchen, I closed the door and rested my head against the cool of the wood. That door was beginning to be a good thinking post for me. In some little part of my brain, I knew I shouldn't be going, but how could something so wrong feel so right?

*****

We drove out on the peninsula—Hemlock Point. The restaurant, a rustic log building, was at the tip of the finger of land with water on both sides. Two torches, flames leaping toward the sky, greeted us at the entrance. Above the door was a carved sign: "TORCHES."

Richly varnished logs graced the ceiling and walls. Intimate tables were scattered everywhere, and along the wall of picture windows were booths with red and white checked tablecloths and high "head resting" benches. Tiny flaming torches enclosed in hurricane glasses stood in the center of each table. The hostess, who seemed to know Robert, seated us in a booth with a magnificent view of Whispering Pine Lake. She set a coloring book and a small box of crayons down for Allyson who immediately busied herself.

"This is really nice," I commented.

"I thought you might like it." Robert seated himself across from me.

The hostess took our drink orders and left.

The sun had just reached the top of the pine trees across the lake, setting a little earlier than at summer's beginning.

"It'll be a fantastic sunset," Robert promised. "And then when it's dark, the restaurant puts on a little show. It's simple. You'll like it."

Our drinks were served along with a coke for Allyson. I stirred the tiny totem pole stick in my drink, caught for a moment with nothing to say.

The young waitress, dishwater blond hair pulled back into a ponytail, began to recite about six selections from memory. Robert suggested the smoked pork chops for me and a northern grilled cheese for Allyson.

As we sipped our drinks, we talked about our lives, skirting main topics like marriage. It was as if Jeb didn't exist, for this moment in time, anyway.

Halfway through our meal, the sky darkened with evening, and Robert pointed out the window to the evening show about to start.

A boy in a rowboat was placing tiny floating torches in glass jars that were tucked into inflated little rafts out on the water near the shoreline. When he finished, he positioned his small boat to easily catch stray torches from escaping into the lake. He gently pushed escapees back with his oar. By this time, the dining room was filled with diners; most of them were watching the silent show from the large picture windows as they ate or sipped drinks.

"Years ago, only a few rowboats and canoes were on these lakes. They all maneuvered around the flaming torches creating quite a show." Robert explained. "I have a feeling this practice may be stopped altogether if the torch boy misses any of the strays."

They put little candles out on the ice, and the skaters went around them. The thought occurred to me.

"Is this place opened in the winter?" I asked.

"No, it closes at the end of October. This building isn't insulated, and it gets rather cold up here," Robert answered as he watched the show.

My thoughts were interrupted by something Robert saw out the window.

"Look, Allyson. That one got away, and he has to chase it."

Allyson stood on her chair and pressed her face against the window.

I looked around the dining room and noticed massive stone fireplaces at opposite ends, darkened in the summer heat.

"When do they have fires in those fireplaces?" I asked.

Robert was still pointing out things to Allyson as he answered, "In the fall, when it cools off."

He turned toward me and touched my hand. "I wish you could be here then. The colors are beautiful."

Tingling sensations traveled from his touch, leaving a glow.

A few moments later, his filled fork posed in midair, he said, "Come to think of it, this place used to be open in the winter. But that was ages ago. It's changed owners once or twice since then."

"Would it have had a different name?" My interest was sparked.

"I don't remember. It might have."

"Would it have been called *Candles*?"

Robert concentrated on his food, and it took him a few bites to answer, "As a matter of fact, I think that was it."

He smiled and looked across the table at me. "How would you know that?"

"Ah—oh, Jeb mentioned it," I lied.

It was an odd feeling to be sitting in the same place, maybe even at the same table as Olivia and Lester did over forty years ago. *Wait until Lisa hears about this*, I thought. Then immediately, I felt a pang of conscience wondering if I should tell Lisa about this dinner date. After all, I did make a promise that I wasn't keeping.

I had two drinks at the restaurant and barely finished the second. Just for a brief moment, I happened to gaze toward the massive fireplace blackened with bygone fires and at an intimate table on the other side of the room sat two people. For some unknown reason, my vision was blurry; but I could have sworn the woman looked eerily familiar to my ghost vision at the end of the pier, even to her dress. She turned to gaze at me. I blinked the blurriness from my eyes to clear them; and in that second, she turned into just another diner, a stranger who had felt my stare and turned to smile at me. I sucked in my breath and pushed my glass away. Was I inebriated enough on two drinks to think I was seeing ghosts? What was wrong with me?

*****

"It was a wonderful dinner. Thank you for being so thoughtful."

I thought it best to thank Robert at the cabin door. He didn't pursue an invitation inside. He thanked me for coming then turned and left. I felt disappointed, but I felt I had done the best thing.

That night, I sat propped against my pillows unable to sleep, again. Being unable to sleep was becoming a habit. Somewhere in my mind, I remembered a song about that; what was it? "A Cheating Heart?" The song popped into my head. *"But sleep won't come the whole night through. A cheating heart will tell on you."*

Robert and Jeb were both on my mind. I was happily married to Jeb; I thought I was. So why did Robert attract me so? I was wise enough to realize that—with the passing of years and the introduction of other responsibilities, namely children—the romance in a marriage may tend to dwindle, and we have to work to rekindle it. I also realized that as imperfect humans, we can be tempted. Scratch that one; sounds too religious. Okay, I need to rekindle romance in my marriage. I liked the sound of that, but how? Did Jeb feel the same? How do I broach that subject without raising suspicion? And then my thoughts turned to Lisa, far above the clouds on her way to

Paris, as I lay sleepless in Olivia's bed. How was I going to do without her company for the next two weeks? Little did I know of the turn of events that would affect my life.

CHAPTER 20

I made myself a cup of Sleepytime tea and sat on the wicker sofa. I thought I spotted something I had not seen previously. I put my cup on the coffee table and went to the window pushing the white laced curtain aside. Why hadn't I noticed this before? Lisa and I had sat on this sofa a countless number of times. There were scratches in the paneling around the window, but they seemed to be only scratches, not a message. Still, they seemed to be deliberately placed there even though they said nothing, looking almost hydrographic. I gazed at them from different angles, running my finger across the rough surfaces. I was sure they looked like they should be saying something. An idea struck me. I got a piece of paper and took the wrapper off of one of Allyson's crayons that had been left under the coffee table. Placing the paper over the scratches, I rubbed it with the broad side of the crayon. It came out on the paper looking like...like mirror writing. Would Olivia have scratched a message backward into the wood? My heart pounding, I took my paper to the bathroom mirror. Sure enough, it was mirror writing!

> e just stopped breathing. he ne er cried.
> earth is frozen. I put him in the old to l box
> in the pantry where it is cold. what do I do now?

"Oh my god!" I whispered to myself. Obviously, this was a message Olivia had felt compelled to write but really hadn't wanted it discovered at all, ever! I felt ill. It was about that dead baby again. She wrote about it twice. And a pantry was mentioned again. I walked the small expanse of the cabin feeling along the walls. There was no pantry. Apparently, there used to be one. But there was not even a nook or corner where one could have been. Maybe it had been destroyed. I wondered who died and was buried in a pantry, of all places. It certainly wasn't Jeb! There was another child. I felt a little better thinking the pantry might be gone, but still, the message disturbed me. What would I have done if I had discovered a pantry? Creepy. I looked hesitantly around the cabin. There had to be many messages. I kept discovering them. When Jeb gets here, we will definitely pick up that bedroom carpet. Might be a book under there. I sat on the couch thinking—a book. That's what I'd do. I'd write a book with all these messages and make up some kind of a story to go with them. Maybe I wouldn't have to make up anything. If I scoured this cabin, I might piece together the whole damn story!

An unexpected knock caused me to jump. Checking my watch, it was 11:30 p.m. I froze, unsure if I should open the door.

"It's me. Robert."

What could he possibly want? But the prospect did excite me.

He filled the doorway dressed in a T-shirt and tan slacks blond hair tousled, a troubled look on his face.

"Robert, what's wrong?"

He put his hands on my shoulders.

"There's been an accident."

"What do you mean, an accident?"

"A plane accident. It was on the news."

At first, I did not understand. Then as realization started sinking in, I felt nauseous. "You don't mean Lisa's plane? Do you?" It was a plea, not a question.

"Maybe it wasn't her plane. They said it was TWA going to Paris."

I grabbed onto the kitchen table, feeling the room sway. Robert put his arms around me.

"What happened?" I whispered.

"They said it exploded about ten minutes after takeoff." Robert spoke quietly.

"Exploded? How? Planes don't explode!"

"I don't have all the details. Why not get Allyson and come with me? It's on television. And we can make some phone calls."

I was in a daze—the mercy of shock and disbelief. Robert was afraid to let go of me. He held onto my arm as I went to wake Allyson. I barely remembered the trip to his home. Once there, I sat in front of the television in disbelief, Allyson asleep on my lap. Robert made phone calls using his influence as a law officer, but what he found out, I didn't want to know. It was Lisa's plane. It was assumed that there were no survivors. That damn plane exploded and crashed into the ocean! Feeling sick, I remembered the message Lisa found on the back of a drawer. I tried not to take it seriously. I talked her out of cancelling her trip. It was my fault.

It is merciful that shocking news doesn't sink in right away. I couldn't cry; I couldn't yell. I could only calmly state, "I have to call Jeb."

"Of course," Robert handed me the phone.

Jeb was hysterical. "I didn't know how to get hold of you. You're coming home, aren't you?"

He never asked how I knew the news being without a television set or from where I was making the call, being without a phone.

"I'll drive home tonight. I should be home about five." I felt weirdly tranquil, like I was just play acting. This wasn't really happening.

Robert took the receiver from me and hung up the phone.

"You're driving home, now?"

"I have to," I answered so calmly that I surprised myself. "Jeb needs me."

"Then I'll take you. You're in no condition to make that long trip by yourself."

He picked up his keys that he had so carelessly thrown on the table.

Surprised at my own control, I said, "You can drive us back to the cabin. I'll pick up my car. Allyson and I have to make this trip by ourselves."

"And why is that?" Robert asked. "You are shocked and appear calm now, but sooner or later, the realization is going to sink in, and if something happened to the two of you, where would Jeb be then?"

I argued, "Jeb knows nothing about you. I can't arrive home with you. We have to do this alone. We'll be fine."

"There's nothing for him to know," Robert said a bit angrily as he picked up Allyson and grabbed me by the arm.

He did drive us back to the cabin, making a few more futile attempts to talk me into letting him drive us to Milwaukee, but when he saw his pleas were useless, he insisted that I wait while he made me a thermos of hot coffee.

"I'm also putting a few cold cans of soda and some ice in your cooler. If you feel tired, hold a cold can on your stomach and then your head. Believe me, it'll wake you up."

He said a few other things, but nothing registered in my brain. In fact, the only thought I could conjure up was how good I would feel when I got home to find out this was all a cruel joke.

*****

The next ten days were torture. My mother took Allyson when Jeb and I traveled to New York to join the other grieving families. I can't honestly say being with the other families helped. It was all so surreal. We were given the information they had for us, but nothing helped the misery. I hated planes. I hated Nicole for inviting Lisa along. I hated the people telling us they shared our sorrow; they didn't. They couldn't possibly know how we felt. I kept silent hoping it was all a mistake.

Once home, we had a funeral Mass for Lisa, minus the remains because there were none. It was as if she never existed. I couldn't concentrate on the service. I couldn't pray. I couldn't think. At times, I didn't believe it. I kept swallowing the imaginary lump in my throat. I couldn't shake it away. My mouth was sour. My eyes pinched. I kept sniffing at the tears until my sniffs couldn't hold them back. I felt shaky like I had gone a week without food. This couldn't be real. Why pray now? The damage was done. Where was God that night?

I seemed to float through the day, surrounded by well-meaning friends and relatives who helped me forget the reality for moments at a time, but when they walked away, the horrible feelings came crashing back. My misery over the loss of Lisa was coupled with my now fear of flying. Returning to work helped Jeb to cope. Often, he put in overtime which may have helped him but not me. I sat in the house filled with pictures and memories of Lisa, accompanied by a three-year-old with little to do but think when I wasn't playing silly little games with Allyson. I tried hard to smile for my youngest daughter and to read her stories without bursting into tears. I know people handle grief in different ways, but I did not understand Jeb's aloofness nor his insistence on working overtime every day. I needed him. I remembered being a family of four, and I needed to share those memories. Allyson didn't understand. She played outside. She watched TV. I didn't want to involve an almost-three-and-a-half-year-old in my grief. She seemed oblivious to our problems, and I wanted to keep it that way for a while. Jeb was avoiding sharing his grief with me. Lisa was his daughter and my stepdaughter. I loved her too. And after all, he did have another daughter who needed him. He wasn't there for us. So when he suggested that Allyson and I return north, I agreed—reluctantly at first, but I agreed. Robert was there. Robert would understand. Didn't he say he had suffered loss? Hadn't he been so comforting that awful night? I had felt more support with him than I was getting from Jeb.

Allyson and I drove alone to Hemlock Bay. But the ride back was not a happy one. Not even the warm sun shining through the windshield could cheer me. How can the sun go on shining as if nothing has happened? I glanced at the families in the passing cars, at the children bouncing in the back seats. Don't those people know there's been a plane crash?

We made a stop for lunch even though I did not feel hungry. My chicken sandwich stuck in my throat. But Allyson seemed to be enjoying her fries, dunking them in ketchup. Next to us was a table with three teenage girls who seemed to be about Lisa's age. They were telling secrets and exchanging giggles while consuming mouthfuls of fries.

They have whole lives ahead of them. I thought. How unfair that Lisa's had to be snuffed out so soon. I turned to gaze out the sunny window to hide my tears. Why, God, why? I prayed. Thousands of planes took off that night. They all landed safely. Why did Lisa have to be on the one that didn't?

"Mommy, why are you crying?" Allyson asked innocently, if not a bit too loudly.

The teenage girls at the next table stopped giggling and peered over at us. Then they turned back to their conversation but without the laughter.

I wiped the corners of my eyes with my napkin. "I was just thinking about Lisa and how much I'll miss her."

"But she said she's coming back with a present for me, remember?"

How I wish I could think as a child. Life would be so much easier. I started to say Lisa won't be coming back, but I choked on the words.

Instead, I said simply, "Finish your fries, honey. We don't want to waste this nice sunny day. Maybe we can get in some swimming."

*****

The woodland drive and the sight of the little brown cabin facing the glimmering lake brought back a flood of memories—the good times of our first weeks. There was an ache in heart. How comforting it would have been to see Robert there waiting for us. Then again, why would he be there? He had no idea that we were returning at this time.

That night, after Allyson was asleep, I roamed the little cabin remembering my last night there—the night of the terrible news. I was so tempted to call Jeb, but I didn't feel I should use Robert's cell phone for my personal call. I thought of calling Robert, but why? My little family wasn't really his concern. I desperately needed someone to talk to, someone who knew my grief. Didn't Robert say that he had lost a child and a wife to an accident? Maybe I should contact him. I started to dial then disconnected.

Life seemed so futile, so short. I cried for Lisa. I cried for Jeb. Then I cried for myself, for I was plagued with the fears that one day Allyson would die and Jeb and Robert and everyone I knew and loved and me. What was life all about, anyway? I remembered my dream that awful night—the fireball that exploded in the sky consuming my children. I feared then that it was a premonition. Did I really believe in those things? To comfort myself, I went to check on sleeping Allyson. She looked so peaceful curled in the snow-white sheets, every bit the angel she was. The sight gave me only momentary relief from my thoughts. Then I complicated things by wondering what would happen to my angel, Allyson, if I left Jeb and sought out Robert? Robert was good with her but would she be shuffled back and forth between me and Jeb? I was getting ahead of myself but it was a thought. I would have to consider it at some point. I closed the bedroom door softly, not knowing where to go or what to do next.

Like ocean waves crashing on rocks, thoughts scattered through my head and crashed in all directions. I could hardly catch my breath. This must be what it feels like to go crazy.

My mind was a jumble of miserable thoughts. I guess recent events had finally caught up to me. Lisa's never coming back. She asked me about canceling her trip. I encouraged her to go! I told her the message had nothing to do with her! It was all my fault. My legs turned to Jell-O; I didn't think they would hold me. I grabbed the kitchen chair for support. I looked through my tears at the boxes Lisa had put on the shelf that first day and relived her excitement at finding that first message. Anger boiled up from a source deep within me. Like a geyser, it erupted into my chest, my arms, my brain. I grabbed the teacup I had left on the table and threw it at the shelf. It hit a cereal box and crashed to the floor, sending tiny white glass pieces, shattering everywhere. I heard a tiny whimper from Allyson's bedroom. A moment of sanity hit me. I thought of Allyson running out with bare feet, stepping on all the glass pieces. I managed to get to the cupboard and get down on my knees to pick up the pieces, which I could barely see through my sheet of tears.

"Ouch." I cut my hand. Blood ran from my palm to make a tiny pool on the floor. I watched it drip. Did Lisa bleed? Did she explode with the plane, or was she alive when the plane hit the water? Did God let her suffer? Had she felt pain or fear? At that moment, I hated him. Why would God let this happen? I was so pissed at God, at myself, at Jeb, at the world!

I came to my senses long enough to find a towel to wrap around my hand and another towel to scoop up the broken pieces.

The thought of Jeb not being there for me in my grief, keeping his misery to himself, stormed into my head. He had been my rock, but he crumbled like sand. I wanted to turn to another man. Robert would show me sympathy. He had been through this. He had been so concerned that fateful night, more concerned about me than Jeb had been.

Why was I now thinking of myself? How selfish I was being. First sending Lisa on that trip, next blaming Jeb when maybe I should be comforting him. But how do you comfort someone who's never there, someone who looks to fishing poles and tennis rackets and equipment sales to hide his misery? Maybe he's crying on his new salesclerk's shoulder. My fist pounded the floor where the glass chips had been, but I had the sense to muffle my scream. I just couldn't deal with a crying Allyson right now. I gulped some air and moved unsteadily toward the wicker sofa. I had to sit down. Putting my head in my uninjured hand, I tried to catch my breath. The air felt like prickles down my throat. What would happen to Allyson if I left Jeb? He'd lose another daughter. She'd lose her daddy. Did I want to leave him? Oh god, what if after all this, he wants to leave me to be with that salesclerk he's crying to? Of course, I wasn't sure of any of this. I just didn't know what to think or how to make sense of anything anymore. Lisa, Jeb, Allyson, Robert, planes exploding, funerals, ghosts—it was all too much. Where was that God when you needed him? Mercifully, sleep overtook me. I crumpled in a heap on the blue cushions of the wicker sofa and let myself drift into oblivion. Oblivion never felt so good.

In the early morning, boat motors humming along the lake were my wakeup call. The sun shinned through the windows reflecting the movement of the water which danced off the ceiling and the walls. It was the promise of a beautiful day. I ached from my night on the couch. I slowly made my way to the door, feeling emotionally drained, and opened it to let in the fresh morning air. It was so relaxing to sit on the porch step in the sunshine for this moment before Allyson woke. I pushed my bare foot through the sand, trying to think of nothing when the sound of a car startled me. It was Robert.

"Steph, how are you?" He called from his open window.

He opened the car door and sat on the step next to me. Respecting my need for silence, he didn't speak for a time and didn't push me to talk. He sensed my need for silence. I really liked him for the aura of comfort he brought with him. Finally, he did speak.

"When did you get back?"

"We got back yesterday afternoon."

I looked not at him but at my hands in my lap. He put his hand over mine.

"I was riding out this way, and I decided to stop. I'm glad I did."

Spirits lifting a bit, I turned to give him a weak smile. "You know, Robert. I'm glad you did too."

It was nice having someone to talk with. We sat over steaming mugs of black coffee, sometimes speaking quietly and sometimes enjoying a moment of silence.

"It's going to be a nice day, a bit cooler but sunny," Robert finally said. "Tomorrow is supposed to be nice also. I can take off tomorrow and let one of my underworked deputies take over." There was an attempt at a giggle. "How about a drive through the National Forest? We'll see some interesting sights."

National Forest. Why did that ring a bell?

"I'd like that," I answered. "And I think Allyson would enjoy it too."

The National Forest, I thought all morning. Where had I heard that before? Then the memory came to me. I hadn't heard about it, I read about it in one of Olivia's messages.

We drove through the National Forest to Billy's home. We made a snowman in Thunder Pass.

Tomorrow would be an interesting day, just how interesting, I had no idea.

CHAPTER 21

I was washing the morning dishes while waiting for Robert. The small window above the sink gave me a vantage point where I could watch Allyson playing in the sandpile right outside the door. I smiled to watch my daughter building with twigs and stones, but then the smile turned to worry. Allyson seemed to be talking to someone. Expecting to see Robert there early, I opened the door. No one was there—no one except Allyson who was happily engaged in three-year-old conversation with thin air.

"Allyson, who are you talking to?"

The child turned with a start at my voice.

"Oh, Mommy, it's my new friend. His name is David."

Then she turned back to her imaginary playmate. "Come back, David," she yelled.

Allyson stood forlorn looking toward the forest.

"Mommy, you scared him. He ran away."

*****

The drive with Robert later that morning was a welcome diversion. The breeze tousled Allyson's hair as she gazed out the open window. We stopped to watch a red fox scoot across the road and into the forest. We stopped at the fish hatchery to gaze at the tanks of minnows being nurtured in a safe environment before having to make it on their own in the lakes. We enjoyed a quick lunch of bologna sandwiches and chips which Robert had so thoughtfully packed. The conversation drifted in and out of the sunlight hours. It didn't touch on Lisa. We carefully avoided any conversation that would mar the beauty of the day, until a small plane flew overhead—a rarity in the Northwoods. The droning motor sound brought back the memories. A wave of anger mixed with sorrow washed over me, making my head pound. *Other planes could fly. Why not the one Lisa was in?* My eyes filled with tears, and I turned away from Robert. Allyson was playing nearby catching grasshoppers. She came running cupping her catch.

I sniffled back my tears as Robert gently touched my arm.

"Why, Robert, why?" I asked tears caught in my throat. "She was so young and so excited. Her life was so full of promise. Why?"

"I don't know why."

He took me in his arms for a brief moment. I would have liked to have stayed there indefinitely. His chest felt warm and welcoming. His arms felt strong—strong enough to ease my fears and calm my anger. But Allyson ran up to us.

"Mommy, Mommy, I got one."

Wiping my eyes with the back of my hands, I turned to look at my child.

"Let's see what you have there," I tried to sound cheerful.

Allyson opened her small hands to reveal the tiny green grasshopper lying still and on his side. She had squeezed too hard in her hurry to show me.

"It's a grasshopper. I think he's sleeping."

I knew better. I just couldn't bring myself to say "dead."

Allyson looked down into her small hands. With all the wisdom of a three-year-old, she said, "I think I squeezed him too hard."

Tears rolled down my cheeks, and I had all I could do to remain silent.

"It's okay, Mommy," my sweet baby girl chimed. "He went to heaven."

Robert took the small dead insect into his own large palm. "Let's give him a proper burial. Yup, that's what we need to do."

The first few moments back in the car were quiet ones. It was as if everyone was lost in thought.

"Mommy," Allyson finally broke the silence, "did we bury Lisa?"

The question was unexpected. Up until this moment, Allyson had persisted in the idea that Lisa was coming home with presents. It was as if she couldn't accept any other explanation. Suddenly an understanding was taking place, or was it an acceptance? But how do you explain to a small child that Lisa's body, like most of the others on the flight, was somewhere in the Atlantic Ocean as yet unfound? That was a difficult concept for me, much less for a three-year-old.

Answer openly. I cautioned myself. It'll make things easier later.

"We had a funeral Mass for her at church. Remember? You were there."

"But did we bury her like my grasshopper?" Allyson demanded.

"Her soul is with Jesus, and she is probably very happy. But we didn't bury her."

"How come?"

I looked to Robert for help. But apparently, he felt this was my territory, for he kept his eyes on the road, not volunteering a thing.

When in doubt, always give the facts as simply as possible.

"The plane went into the ocean."

"You mean she's swimming?"

Oh, how I wished she was swimming. It would be wonderful to think that some plane or boat in the area would discover survivors. But then, it had been three weeks since the accident. What agony to be lost in the ocean and alive for three weeks.

"She's with Jesus."

"Is my grasshopper with Jesus?"

The sun streamed through the pines and maples, brightening the road. Here and there, small lakes glistened between the trees. The summer breeze flowed through the opened windows bringing with it the smell of pine, sand, and water—the smell of peace. What a glorious day to be alive.

"You know what?" Robert said, "I think that heaven is like a great big forest full of lakes and fish and deer and grasshoppers. And it's always warm and sunny there. Just like today."

"Then my grasshopper is there." It was a statement of fact, and it satisfied her.

"Thank you." I mouthed when he smiled at me.

How simple life can be when you are three. I thought. But my mind was troubled—troubled with questions of life and death. Where was Lisa? Was she really anywhere? Does death mean the end of all this—the end of love, of sunshine, of warmth? For that matter, where were Olivia and Lester? They had probably traveled this very road before me. They talked and felt. And where was the infamous Billy, whoever he was? If he was dead like the other players in this little summer drama, could he no longer feel or love? My childhood faith had always sustained me before; teaching me that life as I knew it was temporary but life with faith was eternal. That faith seemed to be failing me now when I needed it the most. I was filled with doubt and despair. *If there isn't more than this,* I thought, *what is the purpose of it all? And what exactly would "more than this" mean?*

An inner voice, clergy in my past perhaps or something I had read, seemed to answer me. *Without doubt, there would be no reason for faith.*

It was Allyson who supplied the faith-filled statement from her storehouse of three-year-old wisdom.

"I bet Jesus gives us little pictures of heaven so we won't be so sad."

"That's really beautiful," Robert exclaimed. "That's what the good things in life must be—little pictures of heaven."

I turned to smile at my daughter. "What a nice thought that was, Allyson."

I wondered if the bad moments were little pictures of hell, but I didn't voice that thought.

"Well, that's what David said."

Robert gazed into the rearview mirror at the curly head cherub in the back seat. "Who's David?"

"He's my friend."

"Allyson has an imaginary friend all of a sudden," I explained.

"He's not *manginary*, he's David, and Mommy scared him away this morning. But he'll be back."

Robert and I looked at each other. I shrugged my shoulders.

"It might be her way of handling the loss," I added but mainly to myself.

I gazed out the window at the endless view of forest and lake, happy to be thinking of something other than death. *We rode through the National Forest to Billy's house.* I sat up and took clearer notice. Olivia and Lester, no, Olivia and Billy had been here. It was almost as if the messages were like a ghost guiding my life this summer, leading me to new places.

"We'll make a stop soon. It's my favorite place in the forest. The area looks as if it doesn't belong here, and it's fun. You'll love it." Robert sounded enthusiastic.

We entered into a picturesque glen of hills and ponds bordered on three sides by forest-covered cliffs. It was strange to see an area of cliffs where the land had been so flat. And Robert was right. It looked as if this glen just didn't belong here.

"Near the end of the ice age, giant icebergs melted leaving rock formations and valleys," Robert explained. "The wind blows through here at times sounding like thunder. That's where the place gets its name: Thunder Pass."

Billy and I built a snowman in Thunder Pass and then... The beauty of the scenery and the knowledge of Olivia and Billy (whomever he was) actually being here sent tingles up and down my spine. I could just imagine the area in winter with fresh fallen snow and ice glistening in the trees.

Robert stopped near a small waterfall cascading over the hill in a magnificent rush, bubbling in foam where it entered the lake. A soft thundering filled the air with nature's music. The water was so clear one could see the pebbles on the bottom where small fish slithered through.

"This place is a glimpse of heaven, for sure." Robert spoke with reverence.

Allyson busied herself throwing pebbles into the lake. I kept a watchful eye on her, at the same time enjoying the splendor of the scene. I was surprised that I felt at peace. It was as if I had stepped out of the real world where planes explode and people die and into a place of serenity and hope. *A sign*, I thought. Surely, it was a sign that Lisa was somewhere beautiful, somewhere peaceful. My serene thoughts wove magic through my being and kept me from feeling

Robert's arms around me until the sound of his voice brought me back to reality.

"This is my favorite place. When life gets hectic or things trouble me, I come here. It puts things back in prospective—for me."

There was no need to answer. I smiled feeling both comforted and awkward with his arms encircling me.

Robert allowed me some long refreshing moments, and then he removed his arms and added with a laugh, "And when I've taken in all the peace I need at the moment, I top it off with a little fun. Come on, I have a terrific place to show you—a change of pace."

A few miles down the road, we came upon an old wood frame building along the water's edge complete with a moving waterwheel. The creaking wood mechanism of the wheel, along with the sloshing sound of the water it moved, rang through the forest. A sprinkling of cars graced the parking lot surrounding the old building.

"For years, this was a working paper mill, but since I was in high school, it became a bar and restaurant—our old hangout."

"THE MILL" was painted in huge black letters on a wooden sign nailed to a tree. Robert pulled into the parking lot.

I was definitely not in the mood for a little fun, as Robert put it. I would rather have stayed in the peace of the forest listening to the falls.

We entered a lofty hall of grayed wood walls that opened into a large room with long narrow windows overlooking the lake and the waterfall. Along the hall walls were pictures of yesteryear, when the place was a working mill. Once inside the open room, I gazed at a ceiling lined with the bottoms of tin drinking cups, each one bearing a name, as Robert ushered us to the square island in the middle of the room that served as the bar.

"What are all those cups on the ceiling?" I asked.

Robert pointed to the cup bottom with "BOB TUCKER" in bold letters.

"They have a special drink here," Robert said. "Pulverizing tonic."

"Sounds delicious."

"It's like a Long Island iced tea on steroids. If you can finish it and stay standing, your cup is hung on the ceiling."

He ordered himself a beer and cranberry juice in a fancy glass for Allyson.

I sat on the tall stool, lifting Allyson to the seat beside me. Looking out the long windows, the day appeared golden as sunset approached. It was surprising how being with Robert lifted my spirits.

"I'll have a pulverizing tonic," I surprised myself. Maybe a Long Island iced tea on steroids would help.

Robert looked startled. "You don't mean it, Steph. I'm warning you. It's lethal."

"I need it." I demanded.

"Give the lady what she needs." Robert winked at the bartender.

My mistake, but this tonic, like a hot flame, burned away my sorrow and depression, leaving ashes of contentment.

The drink was never completely finished. My cup did not receive a place of honor on the ceiling. But enough of it was consumed to create a feeling of euphoria—a much-needed feeling. I guess it was what I needed at that moment. The young evening swam by in flowing peaceful waves. Later, I tried to piece together its events in logical sequence. I remembered juicy steaks on a grill, a roaring fire in a huge stone fireplace, and glasses of red wine. I remembered tucking Allyson into a soft bed, but not her bed, and kissing her good night. I remembered the rush of feeling as I kissed Robert before the roaring fire. It felt like heaven to me. I hadn't realized how desperately I needed to feel alive again. I guess I was drunk both with alcohol and passion. I threw care to the wind and went with my gut feelings. Tender hands rubbed my back as we kissed. He pressed me close as I felt my clothes slip away. Tingling sensations soared through my body. I thought my heart would beat a hole in my chest. I slightly remember him picking me up and carrying me into the bedroom. After that, everything became a heated blur—a nice heated blur of thrilling vibrations. The tonic, the wine, the beauty of this place, and Robert's tender, strong hands wove their magic.

*****

I woke early, when the dark of night gives way to the gray of daylight, before the sun actually rises above the horizon. I was cradled comfortably in Robert's arms amid the soft snow-white wrinkled sheets. I felt exhilarated and warm. Then, like waves in a storm, pangs of shame began to sweep over me. I had been innocent. The only man I ever made love to was Jeb, my husband, until today. I gently lifted Robert's arm from across my body and crept from his bed. I was not innocent any longer. Feeling my nakedness, I searched for my trail of clothes, putting them on as I found them on the floor. Thank god for wrinkle-free fabrics. I chuckled to myself. I made my way into the bathroom, expecting to see the wild, hardened face of a harlot in the bathroom mirror. What I saw surprised me. My face glowed with an inner peace. My eyes shone bright. My skin looked pleasantly tanned. I smiled at my image and splashed my face with cool water. Needing desperately to brush my teeth, I rummaged around the countertop and found a toothbrush. I scrubbed it clean with soap and hot water then used it and replaced it in the holder. I crept quietly into the room where Allyson slept surprised at myself that I remembered where it was. She looked so peaceful asleep that I decided not to wake her. Leaving her room, I turned in search of a coffee pot but walked right into Robert who was standing, smiling behind me.

"Oops, I didn't know you were awake," I tried to excuse myself.

"There was a cold and empty feeling beside me," he answered. "I came in search of warmth."

He grabbed my shoulders and kissed my forehead.

"I hope you're not sorry. I'm not," he whispered.

Then without waiting for my answer, he turned toward the kitchen.

"I'll make us some coffee."

Not sorry, I thought as I followed him. *Am I?* I should be. I had felt shame when I awoke, but now I wasn't sure anymore.

The kitchen was a "dream come true" to me. The walls and ceiling were honey pine paneling. Large bay windows brought in the sunlight—the pine trees, the birds, and a small pristine lake glistening in the distance. An island counter in the center of the room served as a working space and a table. The patio door opened onto the deck overlooking the forest. I remembered being out on this deck watching the steaks on the grill—the memory in a foggy area of my head. I opened the doors and walked into the fresh morning air. The sun rising over the lake warmed every bone in my body. I gazed over the railing at the pebble path below; wild flowers were growing along its borders. The path led into the forest and came out near the lake in the distance. I felt like God must feel looking down at His creation. Then a disturbing thought occurred to me: it was in a message I had read. *You could see for miles around at Billy's cabin.*

Robert brought out a cup of steaming brew.

"How are you feeling this morning?"

"Are you implying I drank too much?"

"Well and that."

"I actually feel rather good considering I had my first—what was that drink again? Pulverizing Tonic and several glasses of red wine. What the heck was in Pulverizing Tonic?" I laughed.

He touched his coffee cup to mine as a toast of sorts and smiled.

"It's a secret, a love potion of some sort."

"Ah," I took a slow swallow from my warm cup and returned his smile. "That explains a lot."

"Mommy," I heard from inside.

"Out on the porch, sweetie."

Robert turned to go inside. "Morning, Shortie. I'm going to make us some pancakes and eggs."

We watched him pull down a large frying pan from the array of pots and pans that hung in a circle above the island counter.

"Hope you like omelets," he called out to me. "I make a wicked one."

The butter sizzled, filling the air with its sweet aroma. He brought a glass of orange juice out for Allyson. While he cooked, Allyson and I explored the beautiful home I had not noticed the night before. Guess I had other things on my mind. Or maybe I was mindless. The living room faced the west. A ceiling to floor window overlooked the forest and another lake in the distance. Sunsets must be lovely here. Did we get here in time to see one? Funny, I couldn't remember.

A soft white rug lay in the center of a highly polished wood floor. Green leather furniture faced the massive fireplace. Above the seating area, the cathedral ceiling arched suspending a wagon wheel with lights in hurricane glasses. A rope with a wooden Swiss mountain climber dangled from the center of the wheel. How unique! I'll have to ask Robert about that light. But, in my search of the room, it was the fireplace wall that attracted my attention. It was flanked with a raw piece of wood for a mantel, several photographs in silver frames resting on it. There was a picture of Robert in a football uniform, looking much thinner. There was Robert in a cap and gown beaming with pride. And, an older couple, arms about each other, the gentleman resembling Robert. His parents? My fingers ran across the mantle. Then I took a quick span of the room. Where were pictures of his wife and child? There were none. This obviously had been his parent's home. I wondered if they were still living. This was not the home Robert had brought me to the night of the plane crash.

"Mommy, this isn't our cabinet."

"Cabin, cabin," I corrected with a smile. "And no, we're not at home. We're here because it got too late to go home."

I wondered what Allyson would register and blab to her dad. I had to come up with an explanation if she did. One "fall from grace" breeds another. Now I might have to be dishonest with Jeb. What were my choices?

"This isn't Robert's house neither," Allyson replied.

Robert poked his head into the living room.

"Breakfast is served."

I grabbed the picture of the older couple as we walked to the breakfast bar.

A scrumptious feast was set featuring omelets shiny with melted butter. I noticed that Robert's hair was in place, looking neat as usual except for those stray blond wisps which hung over his forehead giving him his youthful appearance. A dark blue terry cloth robe tied snuggly at his waist opened slightly at his chest revealing wisps of blondish hair.

Blue certainly becomes him, I chuckled to myself, the color of his chosen profession.

"Thought Shorty might like her eggs scrambled."

"You said pancakes," Allyson whined.

"And pancakes too." He placed another plate in front of her.

I put the silver framed photograph on the breakfast bar.

"I was wondering, are these your parents?"

Robert glanced at the picture. "Yes, they are. Don't I look a bit like dad?"

"This man sure appears to be an image of you or you an image of him. Are they still living, Robert?"

"My father built this home. I bought it from him when they moved into a retirement condo in Minnow Point. It's my escape, my paradise, and will probably be my retirement home." He poured us both another cup of coffee.

Well, that explains where I am. I thought.

"Yes, they are living. And very happily, I might add. They have tons of activities and friends at the condo village. It's been great for them."

I made a decision not to ask about the absence of pictures of his family. I would ask later. Maybe it had been more difficult for Robert to adjust than I had originally thought.

As I took bite after bite of the expertly prepared omelet, a strange memory occurred to me. *We built a roaring fire in the fireplace. That's when I let Billy make love to me.* I was lost in thought. They had come through Thunder Pass and built a snowman. Thunder Pass. I thought of the beautiful glen that had brought me so much peace. I imagined it iced over with winter snow. Was the water in the falls moving or frozen still when Olivia and Billy built their snowman? Could this be—the very house they came to?

"A penny for your thoughts." Robert smiled.

"More eggs, please." Allyson held up her empty plate.

"Coming right up."

"Wow, Allyson. You've never asked for seconds of eggs before. They must be good."

"I make 'em the best, don't I?"

"I like Robert's eggs. Daddy never makes eggs."

It was the word *daddy* that brought me back to reality. There were those pangs of guilt again. What would Allyson let slip to Jeb? How could something wrong feel so good?

I watched Robert's easy manner with Allyson. Did he take advantage of my grieving situation and all that alcohol I consumed? Or was this something I wanted also? Was I acting like my notorious mother-in-law?

"As I said, a penny for your thoughts," Robert whispered into the silence.

"Oh, I was just wondering, what's your father's name?" I surprised myself with the question.

I hadn't really planned to ask it, but it was the first thing that came to mind as I tried to avoid voicing my real thoughts.

"His name is William."

"William? Is he called William?" My heart sank.

"By some, but the town called him Billy."

If there was shock on my face, Robert didn't wait to see it. He was already cleaning up our dishes as Allyson finally took a single bite of her pancake.

"It's Sunday, you know," he said. "And there's this pretty little chapel in the woods we can go to. It will really give you a flavor of faith in the Northwoods."

He wiped the table clean in front of us. "And we all could use a little flavor of faith," he added. He looked up at my face with the frozen smile.

Somehow, attending church did not seem to fit in with an affair. What an interesting man Robert was turning out to be.

"I—we have nothing suitable to wear."

"Up north, it's come as you are. Jeans, even shorts are fine. You and Allyson will look great."

Robert was right about the flavor of faith. Down the forest road, not far from his "paradise" home stood the small log-hewed chapel topped with a steeple and super piercing bell. It was ringing by the time we arrived. The sides of the building boasted long screened-in windows, more like a porch. Wooden benches were already filling with worshipers. A rather large pine cone cross was the only decoration hung on the front wall, and the smell of old wood and forest vegetation permeated the air.

People were smiling and friendly as we were seated.

"Services are held here from Memorial Day to Labor Day. People of all faiths come to hear a different preacher each week." Robert whispered in my ear.

The name "Billy" echoed in my mind as the entire congregation raised its voice in song. The trees vibrated with the very essence of the music. The sun streamed through the windows warming the small congregation. Behind the altar was a large glass window brushed by the gentle boughs of pine trees. I should have been in peace here. I was not.

It had been a long time since I had been to church, except for Lisa's memorial mass. Somehow, our hectic lives caused us to eliminate that practice. Sunday became a day to sleep in. I had been concerned about the children having some sort of faith. I tried to read Bible stories to them occasionally and help them get in the practice of night prayer. But even that had fallen by the wayside. I had forgotten how uplifting and comforting faith could be. But I didn't feel uplifted or comforted at the moment. I had lived through an interesting day—a very romantic evening. One side of me felt overjoyed, the other shameful, and it was all washed in sorrow and grief. What a mix! I gazed at Robert, handsome creature, lifting his voice in song. But all I could think of was Lisa and exploding planes and Olivia and Billy and Robert's father having the same name. Was he *the* Billy? And where are pictures of Robert's wife and child? And was Robert taking advantage of my weaknesses? And what kind of person was I to so easily be led into an affair? And what if we hadn't taken any precautions and I had his child? My mind was a jumble of questions all through the service.

As the congregation bowed its head in prayer, conflicting thoughts filled my head. My old faith had taught me well. Marriage vows were "until death do us part," not "until a ghost leads me elsewhere." I giggled a bit at my thought. Becoming suddenly serious, I remembered my hate of God during my "meltdown" a few days ago. I felt bad about that. If I believed in signs, he sure had given me enough of them. First that message Lisa found that had her concerned about her trip, then the difficulty we had getting to Milwaukee with the tornado and all. But would that have stopped a logical person? Probably not. I guess life is what it is. I wasn't really tuned in to the sermon, but I did catch parts of it. It was something about God giving us free will, the right to choose, and our choices carried consequences. God didn't will us evil. We, more or less, did it to ourselves. But how did I cause the plane crash? I didn't. It was very confusing. God was loving, the minister preached. He would help us overcome the bad. Then I heard him say something very profound. He said it was a quote he had read, but it suited his sermon. That quote made all the difference to me.

"God never said the journey would be easy. He said the arrival would be worthwhile."

I guess if God gave us life and love, how could I be angry with him? Was he angry with me when I threw care to the wind and did what I wanted to do? I sighed and stared at the pine cone cross and the pine branches brushing against the small square window above it. I guess all our lives on earth are temporary anyway. We need to set our sights on the eternal. I guess.

I imagine I got a lot more out of that sermon than I originally thought, or were those just my thoughts as the preacher was preaching? The thoughts brought fresh tears—tears of confusion, tears of sudden realizations. I dabbed my eyes with a tissue and willed the tears away. All of a sudden, I craved an overpowering desire to know all. Knowledge saves. I thought. Possibly, knowing all would help me make better decisions. Sometimes I despised myself for being so wishy-washy. Other people seemed able to make a decision and go with the plan, not me. I overthought everything! Am I wrong? Am I right? My gosh, I had a difficult time deciding if I should buy a pair of shoes in black or red. I'd break into a sweat in the store just making a decision. Then the worst part, I'd second-guess myself after my decision was made! My goal from now forward was to be more decisive. I wondered if I could pull it off?

Please, God, help. There I said it: a prayer. Would it be answered?

"Well, we have the day ahead of us. What would you like to do?" Robert asked as he started the car.

I volunteered, "I'd like to drive to Minnow Point. I'd like to meet your parents."

My first attempt at being decisive. It felt good.

If surprised, Robert didn't show it. "Your wish is my command."

Then he added, "Minnow Point has some interesting little shops and a few wonderful restaurants. We could eat lunch there. In fact, I might suggest that mom and dad come with us, if you don't mind."

"I don't mind at all. But how will you explain Allyson and me?"

Robert smiled. "Good question." He thought a moment. "You're the wife of a friend. Your husband is home on business, and I took you and your daughter to church."

"Believable, I guess."

"What do you mean, believable? It's the truth."

CHAPTER 22

Minnow Point was not the sleepy little town its name might imply. Its streets were lined with unique gift and novelty shops and tons of summer tourists. Robert bought Allyson some fudge in the candy shop with the mechanical baker in the window stirring a huge copper pot. The sweet smells were intoxicating.

We explored an antique shop appropriately named Yesteryear where I rummaged through the vintage magazine issues as Robert explained the workings of the old toys to Allyson.

I bought Allyson a T-shirt at Shirts 'n Things, and Robert insisted that she have her own tom-tom from Walk-on-Teepee.

"Boy, you are going to be sorry you bought that." I laughed.

As noon approached, we drove to Minnow Point Retirement Village.

"I should have called them," Robert said. "They love surprises, but they may have eaten lunch already."

Allyson thumped on her tom-tom.

"Well, I'm not really hungry yet. And Allyson has filled up on fudge. So maybe we could visit and then have a late lunch or early supper."

"Great idea."

Minnow Point Retirement Village was a complex of four con-dominium buildings built along a central courtyard on the shore of Minnow Lake. The lake was small and no motorboats were allowed on it, which made it a peaceful retreat. The entrance hall was adorned with a wagon wheel lamp hanging from the highest point on its cathedral ceiling, but the lamp was a much smaller scale than the one in Robert's house. We were greeted by the receptionist who seemed to know Robert. It made me glad that he seemed to be a regular visitor. It showed character.

"I think your parents are in their apartment," the receptionist said. "Let me ring for them."

She talked on the phone in a quiet, pleasant voice. "Go right in Mr. Tucker."

The three of us walked through the double glass doors, Allyson thumping on her new tom-tom, along the green carpeted hallway. At the end, a door flung open, and a pleasant gentleman, a bit older than the picture on the fireplace mantle, stepped out into the hallway.

"Robert," he embraced his son.

"Dad, I want you to meet the family of a friend of mine." It was all the explanation needed.

William Tucker was tall like Robert. He still had a full head of hair, but it was snow white with a few blond streaks. His face was weathered and old, but his features resembled Roberts. I realized that I was probably meeting the secretive Billy of cabin wall fame. Wait until I tell Lisa. Then immediately, the pang of sorrow tugged until I thought I might break out in tears in front of this elderly gentleman.

Swallowing the lump in my throat, I managed to say, "Good to meet you, Mr. Tucker."

William stooped to look at Allyson who hid shyly, slightly behind me. The tom-tom quiet at last.

"Martha, come and look at this precious little package."

As we walked into the apartment, Martha could be seen sitting stately in her wheelchair. She looked younger than her husband even though she was wheelchair bound. Hair fell in soft white ringlets about a cheery face. She put out her arms, but Allyson avoided them. Martha acted unaffected by this show of shyness from a young child.

"Would you like something to eat?" she offered.

"Actually, we came to take the two of you to lunch."

"We eat lunch early around here, remember," Martha chided her son. "We ate at eleven."

"In that case, we'll visit, and the two of you can join us for an early supper about three or so," Robert said.

Our visit included a tour of the complex. Allyson had a chance to wade in the lake which delighted her to no end. It was the only time she gave up the tom-tom willingly. Martha served cookies and lemonade on the outdoor patio. Allyson showed her growing hunger by taking several cookies.

Conversation was light and centered mainly about the interesting summer weather and the tornado of a few weeks ago. Nothing was mentioned of Lisa or the ill-fated flight, much to my relief. They talked about the summer Olympic Games in Atlanta. Evidently, Robert's parents were avid Olympic watchers.

"If football was an Olympic sport when Bobby was young, he would have made the team." It was interesting to hear him refer to his son as Bobby.

I watched the older Mr. Tucker. I saw many similarities between him and his son. It was easy to see how Olivia had been taken with him.

"I guess it's almost time for that early supper." Robert laughed.

I helped Martha collect plates and cups to take into the small kitchen. I was surprised at how agile and independent Martha was in her wheelchair. This gave us a moment alone as well—a moment for some questions.

"Robert told me that he never had a serious girlfriend after his wife died. Is that true?"

Martha wheeled herself to the sink counter which had been lowered to accommodate the wheelchair.

"Wife?" she asked. "Robert never was married, much to our disappointment."

"You mean he didn't have a son?"

"Did he tell you he did?"

I wanted more information without sounding as if I were prying. Admitting that Robert might have lied to me might silence his mother. I took a moment to decide on my strategy.

"I must have misunderstood. I thought he mentioned a wife and son. He did talk about a car accident."

Martha turned her chair to face me. Her eyes were misted with tears of memory.

"There was a car accident. Sara was Robert's fiancée. They were to be married in June. But she was killed in May." Martha ended the dialogue with, "There haven't been any other serious women in my Robert's life, as far as I know."

*****

As usual, Allyson fell asleep on the way home. We had a pleasant supper with his parents. Talk was limited and quiet. I felt limited and quiet. Lisa's death, thoughts of the night before, and the realization that Robert had lied to me about a wife and child played heavily on my mind. How would I approach Robert's lies to me? Why had he lied?

I watched him, intent on driving the car as the sun set, leaving the forest road in semidarkness.

"You seem absorbed in thought," Robert broke the stillness. "Is there something I could help you with?"

I looked at him. "Actually, yes there is. You could clear up something that is bothering me."

"Yes, I did use protection. You don't have to worry."

"What? Oh yes, good, I mean I'm glad you did. I did think of it and worry a bit, but that's not what I am presently thinking of."

Robert gave me a quick inquisitive glance then looked back to the road. "I'm all ears and ready to help," he said too confidently.

"Robert, you told me you were married and had a son."

He was quiet for what seemed to be a long while. Then he said, "And my mother told you something else."

"Yes, she did."

"What did she tell you?"

I was demanding, "No, you explain first."

Robert took a deep breath. "I was never married. I was engaged. My fiancée ran her car off the road into one of the lakes about a month before our wedding."

"And there was no son?" It was more a statement than a question.

"There was a child, her child, not my child. My parents never accepted the fact that I was marrying a woman with a child. The boy was in the car with her. He was drowned as well."

We sat in silence for a few moments. Could I believe him now? He sounded convincing, but he had sounded convincing before. I gazed at him.

"Why did you tell me you were married and had a child?"

"Oh, I don't know. Maybe I wanted it to be true." He looked at me. "I also had the feeling, at the time, that it would make me seem safer to you. I felt as if you were contemplating refusing my offer to go for a boat ride."

It was fair enough. I breathed a sigh of relief. I willed myself to accept his explanation because I wanted to. It actually wasn't a lie, I guess. He had just stretched the truth a bit.

"Nothing but the actual truth from now on." He declared.

This was the only time Robert had seemed even close to vulnerable. It made him more human and less the figure of super strength and wisdom that I had attributed to him. *Reality will make our relationship more secure*, I thought. Our relationship, should it be happening? Silence hung like webs in the car. Allyson was still sleeping, and to be honest, I didn't know what else to say. I still felt warmed by the night before but pierced with shame for my lack of control and slightly betrayed by my recent discovery. I gazed at Robert's profile against the darkening sky and felt a stir, some primeval emotion tugging around my heart. I turned back to the road illuminated by the headlights as the car wound its way through the forest. *It shouldn't be happening*, I kept repeating to myself.

"Am I forgiven?"

Robert's voice broke my reverie, and I had to think for a second. What did he just say to me? I jumped as he placed his warm hand over mine.

"Steph? Hello."

I turned to face him, but his features were shrouded in darkness, and he did need to turn back to the road.

"I'm sorry," I mumbled, "I guess I was just lost in thought."

He turned back to me briefly. "Am I forgiven?"

"What? Oh, forgive you? Yes, I do, of course." How could I not forgive him? He was being so nice, so loving. I watched his handsome profile. He became a shadow as he drove in the twilight, but I could make out the outline of his face. The wisps of blond hair that spread across his forehead took on a light of their own in the weak rays of moonlight that flowed through the forest trees.

His grip tightened on my hand.

"Look, I really care for you. It was not my intention to be dishonest. In fact, I almost had forgotten about the statement I made when we first met. I was just hoping to keep you interested. You seemed to be so alone, stuck without a boat, without adult company, and I was trying to extend my hospitality, but I didn't want to give you the wrong idea. I'm sorry. Nothing but truth from now on. Scout's honor!"

And he turned to give me a smile and a mock salute.

I laughed. "Go on. You probably were never a scout."

"I was. I was. For all of two weeks, anyway."

The melancholy mood was broken. He went on to tell me how his father had insisted that every American boy needs scouting experience. Then shortly after joining came the initiation camping weekend. It rained buckets the first night out in the open, and his tentmate dared him to touch the inside of the tent causing it to become completely drippy 'till he was soaked. In the morning, he woke to find that a bear had visited the camp and consumed whatever food was left. On and on, he spun his tale until I laughed with him, and we arrived at the cabin in a much easier mood. In fact, the mood was too easy.

He was out of the car before I was, carrying a sleeping Allyson to bed. He took me in his arms, and we kissed 'till I felt stars shooting out of my head. It was difficult, but I pulled away.

"I can't. I just can't."

"What is different from last night?" he asked.

"Well, pulverizing tonic and wine for one thing."

"You mean I appeal to you only when you are a bit inebriated?"

"That's not fair, Robert. You appeal to me, all right. But my moral sense kicked in. I'm married. I'm so confused right now. You're beginning to mean so much to me, and I'm not sure how I feel about my husband anymore. I-I need a some time to digest all of this. Please give me a little time tonight."

He kissed my forehead and gave me a tender hug.

"I understand. I may not like it but I do understand."

It was painful to watch him drive away. He was so nice, so understanding. I was really beginning to love that man. I had experienced that before, with Jeb in the time before Robert.

I wasn't sure how happy I was with my decision, but I felt a little like I was making up for last night. And I actually made a decision. I started to wonder if it was the right decision. I really did want him to stay. Then I told myself to stop; a decision made is a decision made. I actually proclaimed that out loud. My grown-up self was kicking in. It felt liberating.

I fell into a sound sleep only to be awoken by Allyson coming into my room, crying. I took her under the covers, thankful that Robert was not there.

"What's the matter, honey? Was the day too busy for you?"

Between sobs, Allyson murmured, "David came. And he said I had a terrible day. He said my mommy wasn't being nice. And I should stay here and play with him and not always be going away."

I held my small daughter close.

"It was only a dream, honey, only a dream. David is a dream."

Allyson picked her little head up indignantly, "David is real. And he really said that!"

"*Okay, okay,*" I padded her. "Guess what? Tomorrow we'll stay here and play."

She seemed satisfied and finally fell back to sleep. Carefully, I returned her to her bed and tucked the sheet around her chin. But now, I could not sleep, as usual.

David had told her that I wasn't being nice. What did David mean? Damn, I knew what he meant! Wait a minute! David was a figment of a three-year-old imagination. Why should I care what a stupid nobody said?

Just because he lived in the cabin wall gave him no power to condemn me. I actually giggled at my last thought. But then, I realized I was wide awake and feeling the urge to search for more messages from Olivia. Maybe there was something I had overlooked, and I could find something, any little thing to hold on to—some word of advice or perhaps a glimpse into the future that might help me to alter events. I felt myself getting obsessed. I looked every place I hadn't looked before, and I even looked in some of the old places to reread what was there. I took the drawers out of the dresser in my bedroom and moved the heavy wooded furniture to look behind it as Lisa had done. I was like a woman on a mission, but nothing turned up. Nothing. I couldn't find any more messages, just the old ones. Possibly, there were some under my bedroom carpet, but those would have to wait. I was alone. Or was I? I was beginning to ponder, was I looking to ghosts to make choices for me? Or was I using the ghosts and the messages to eliminate my feelings of guilt, not my fault, so to speak.

I tried to remember when I stopped asking God to help. As I slowly refilled and replaced the drawer, I breathed a prayer. *Please, God, help. Was that you who helped me refuse Robert tonight? Now please help me rekindle my romance with Jeb, if even a smidgen of romance remains. And please, please, God, help me to come to grips with Lisa. Help me to truly believe she is with you. Help me to go on. Help me not to hate you. I don't want to hate you. I need peace. And help me to relax. My obsession is driving me wild. Please help.*

CHAPTER 23

Monday morning dawned warm and sunny. I was determined to occupy Allyson's time so as not to allow any visits from David. I feared my daughter's need for an imaginary friend as much as I feared the friend.

"Let's make lunch together," I suggested after a morning of swimming and playing in the sand. "What would you like?"

"Peanut butter and jelly."

Why ask? I should have known.

"Mommy, you make lunch. I'll play outside."

"I'll agree provided you play by the back door. And you stay right there!" I watched my daughter from the kitchen window as I put together the sandwiches.

I left the window momentarily to get the banana cake from the refrigerator. When I returned, Allyson was nowhere in sight. I called for her, but there was no response.

My god, I thought, *how long was I gone?* Thirty seconds? A minute? Where could she have gone?

I ran to the lake. "Allyson, Allyson."

A water skier flew by sending a spray of foam that rippled to the shore. But there was no little girl in view. Wild with fear and panic, I ran back to the cabin to get the cell phone.

"Mommy, I'm right here."

Allyson came walking out of the woods. Relief then anger flared in my head. I grabbed my daughter by her little shoulders and shook her.

"I told you to stay right here next to the cabin. Where have you been?"

Allyson began to cry. "You're hurting me, Mommy."

I let go of her shoulders and hugged her instead.

"I didn't mean to hurt you, honey. I was just so scared. Where were you?"

"I walked in the woods," Allyson said between sobs.

"But I told you to stay right here." I stooped to be at eye level with her. "Never, never, walk in the woods alone."

"But I wasn't alone," Allyson pleaded. "David was with me."

*****

Going to town for the afternoon seemed like a sensible idea— anything to get Allyson away from the cabin for a while. Oh, she didn't want to go, insisting that David wanted her to stay put, and I promised. That only made me more determined. I promised her that maybe we'd see Robert, and he'd have a fun surprise thing to do. The cell phone lay on the seat between us, and it scared me half to death when it rang.

"Hi, Steph, thought I might interest you in driving into town for an hour or so."

"Believe it or not, I'm on my way. What did you have in mind?"

"Meet me at the Old Curiosity Shop. Grab a booth and order me the cinnamon coffee if I'm not there when you arrive. I have about thirty minutes to kill."

"Sounds good. Where is the Old Curiosity Shop? I don't remember seeing it."

"About two minutes north of Torches on the point. You won't miss the building. It looks like an old curiosity shop."

"I'll be there, Robert."

Glad for a destination since none had been planned, I placed the cell phone on the seat and drove with new purpose. There was something exciting about the prospect of seeing Robert again, and Allyson was happy when I told her.

As I drove, I questioned her about the imaginary friend.

"Where does David live, Allyson?"

"He lives in our cabin, Mommy, in the wall."

"Right. In the wall." I swerved a bit on the road as I looked at my daughter's innocent face. What do I ask next?

"Isn't it kind of spooky living in a wall?"

Allyson shrugged her shoulders. "Don't know. I guess."

"Well, does he tell you anything about his home in the wall?" I felt foolish. But, after all, I was carrying on a conversation with a three-year-old.

"Nope."

I saw I was getting nowhere fast.

"Well, is he happy living in the wall?" I looked at Allyson's profile before staring back at the road. Tight and tiny blond curls hugged her face as she turned to me with pleading hazel eyes and puffy baby cheeks. How I loved her!

"He's happy when he plays with me. When are we going back to the cabinet, Mommy?"

"Cabin, Allyson, cabin. You just said it right a minute ago. And we should be back by supper time."

"David will be sad today." And she slumped back against her seat.

"It'll give him a chance to play some games with his mommy in the wall." I thought I was being clever.

I looked at my daughter, feigning a smile. Allyson was turned away, looking out her window.

*****

Robert was right. The building did look like an old curiosity shop just as the name suggested. It was built of sand-colored brick—the only building on the point, not of wood. There was an arched entrance door opened to let in the summer air. Two matching arched windows on either side of the door were made with brown, green, and amber glass bottle bottoms cemented together to form unique colored patterns. When my eyes became accustomed to the dim light within, I was fascinated with the multicolored patterns of light streaming through the windows. I scanned the room for Robert and not seeing him, I found the wall of booths and secured an empty one.

"May I take your order?"

I was startled that the waitress had appeared so quickly.

"Ah, yes, we're expecting someone to join us. He would like a cinnamon coffee, and I'll just have your regular hearty roast. What would you recommend for a child?"

"Our chocolate milk is a favorite. It's whipped with cinnamon and a touch of vanilla, and it comes with a dab of chocolate ice cream. Kids love it."

"Does that sound good to you, Allyson?"

Allyson shook her head affirmatively.

The waitress returned with the order before Robert arrived.

"I'm sorry. I didn't expect you back so fast. Could you hold the cinnamon coffee until my friend arrives? I wouldn't want it to get cold."

"Of course." She removed Robert's cup and left.

Allyson busied herself dunking the scoop of ice cream in her milk with a spoon.

"Have you seen that Beinfield woman?"

Hearing my name mentioned, I looked around. Realizing that I was overhearing conversation in the booth behind me, I sat back until my ear pressed the back of my bench.

"No, I have no idea what she looks like, but I hear she's a bit like our famous Mrs. Beinfield. It must run in the blood."

"You can't say it runs in the blood, Helen. The Beinfield woman would be a daughter-in-law."

"Oh, that's right. She had a son. What was his name?"

"I think his name was Jeremy or something like that."

"No, Jeffery, Jeff. Or something odder. Jeb, Jeb, that's what they called him. I remember he was a weird little kid."

"Well, no wonder, with a mother like that."

Allyson interrupted, "Mommy, I can't get any ice cream. It keeps sinking. Watch."

She pushed the frozen lump with her spoon and giggled as it popped back up in the milk.

"I'll help you but, shh, I'm trying to hear something," I whispered as I took my daughter's spoon and tried to grab a spoonful of the stuff myself.

I was unsuccessful at first which caused Allyson to giggle, but eventually, I managed a spoonful which I handed to her. In the process, I missed some of the conversation behind me.

"Bobby's on the prowl. He'll get that old Beinfield kid paid back."

Damn. What did I miss? I wondered. I leaned further back in the booth.

"Mommy, get some more on." Allyson handed her spoon to me.

I reluctantly moved the ice cream to the side of the glass with the spoon and managed a spoonful of the creamy stuff on my first try. I handed the spoon to Allyson.

"I hear he's really got that new Beinfield woman all a dither. And she's falling for it."

"Quite a womanizer, that Bobby."

The waitress appeared at the booth behind me ending the conversation. Apparently, the check was presented and paid. I felt the bumps as two people scrambled out of the booth. I turned to see two elderly ladies waddle to the door, giggling like school girls sharing a secret. My heart sank.

"You beat me."

Robert appeared from the other side of the room. It took some maneuvering settling his athletic bulk between the darkly polished table and bench of the booth.

"Hi, Shortie, I see you're enjoying the famous chocolate milk."

"Hi, Robert, can you help me get some ice cream?"

"Sure, Shortie. I got this move down pat. Watch me."

He scooped up a large spoonful and fed it to her.

"Those old town biddies just walked out the door. Wonder what they were giggling about?" Robert remarked, raising his eyes to the door over Allyson's spoon.

"They were laughing about *Bobby* taking advantage of the new Beinfield woman."

Robert looked truly remorseful. "Oh, I'm sorry. I'm sorry you had to hear that. They didn't know who you were, did they?" Then before I had a chance to answer, he continued. "No, of course they didn't. But if they had, it wouldn't have stopped them. They would have delighted in upsetting you."

He reached to grab my hand, but I pulled away.

"They got the information somewhere. It seems that you might have been dishonest with me again."

The waitress came with Robert's coffee. "You want a refill, Miss?"

I shook my head, no, afraid that voicing the word might bring me to tears. I felt angry and humiliated.

"Steph," Robert ignored his coffee cup. "We've both been dishonest with each other."

Without him having to say another word, I knew that he knew that I knew more than I had told him.

"Look, I got some myself." Allyson broke the awkward moment with her spoon full of ice cream.

"That's nice, honey."

"Good work, Shortie."

I turned my full gaze on Robert and asked with all the innocence I could muster. "What do you mean we both have been dishonest?"

"You know more about what happened and with whom than you've been letting on. I don't know if that husband of yours told you anything. I'm not sure he even knew the whole of it. So I don't know where you got your information. But I'm sure you know."

Robert puckered his lips in thought, looking toward the door for a brief second then back at me.

"Of course, you weren't really being dishonest. I never asked you if you knew anything, so why should you tell me about it?" He stated much softer.

"Robert, I have to know." I was surprised my voice sounded so in control. I certainly didn't feel that way. "Was all the attention you've given me an effort to pay back the Beinfields for the trouble they apparently caused forty years ago?"

We both startled at the new noise. Allyson had put her straw in the glass and was blowing bubbles in the milk.

"Allyson, stop that." I angrily took the straw from the child's mouth and laid it on the table. "Drink the milk or eat the ice cream with your spoon. You know better."

Unconcerned, Allyson drank some of the milk, laughing when the remainder of the ice cream hit her in the nose. Feeling uncomfortable with my anger at my child, I wiped Allyson's nose with the napkin and handed back the straw.

"I'm sorry, honey. It's just that Robert and I are talking, and we didn't like all that silly noise. You can use your straw. Just don't blow bubbles, *okay?*"

"I'm going to be very honest with you, Steph."

I gave my attention back to Robert, almost afraid at what I would hear.

"I had no intention of paying anybody back for anything. It's just that…well…"

He appeared uncomfortable. He took a sip of his coffee in an effort to gather his thoughts. It was so unlike him. I waited for him to continue.

"People saw me with you that night at *Torches*. They asked about you. I made the mistake of telling them who you were. I didn't share the fact that you were married. I don't even know if they surmised that. I just winked and let them think what they wanted, I guess, knowing they might think that I was seeking some kind of revenge. I wasn't, of course, but I wanted to appear on top of things in their eyes. In fact, it was stupid. But you don't know this town."

I didn't know how to take this information.

"Robert," I finally said, "You don't seem to be the kind of man who would care what the town thinks of you. So I don't really buy your story."

He held fast to his coffee cup and seemed more determined than contrite at the moment.

"Sheriff is an elected position in this town. I like my job. I don't want to get on the voter's bad side. If it wasn't for that, you would be right. I wouldn't give a damn what they thought."

"Robert said a bad word." Allyson looked up, milk mustache on her upper lip.

"Sorry, Shortie, I meant darn. Is that better?"

"Is *darn* better, Mommy?"

"Darn is better, dear."

I breathed deeply. There was so much to say, so much to ask. Where should I start?

Robert took the sigh as a change of heart. He reached out and touched my hand. I did not pull away this time, but I didn't relax either.

"Look, Robert, if you're so worried about your image, why do you continue to be with me?"

"Good question." He removed his hand and appeared thought-ful. "You know what? I really enjoy your company. You're the first I can honestly say I want to be with in the last ten years. I've grown to have real feelings for you. I'm sorry. I really am. I want us both to be nothing but honest from now on. Please believe me when I tell you that my relationship with you is pure attraction. I wouldn't be so trite to try to pay someone back for something that happened forty years ago. It was between my dad and your in-laws. It had nothing to do with you." He held my hand and squeezed it. "Am I forgiven?"

"Then your dad was Olivia's Billy."

"You knew you had that one figured out," he answered softly.

His eyebrows curled and his root beer brown eyes were intoxicating.

I'm really losing it. He's so damn attractive—to me.

There were other questions to ask but his "thirty minutes to kill" were up, and Allyson was restless.

"Mommy, I have to go to the potty."

"It's okay," Robert said. "I have to leave."

I stood to take my daughter to the restroom. Robert rose as a polite gesture and pointed to the back of the shop.

He grabbed my arm before I could leave. "Steph?"

"All's forgiven?"

Allyson slid out of the booth, past Robert. She grabbed my hand.

"I have a lot more questions, Robert. They need answers."

"I have to get back to work. I'll be over tonight, about nine? Will that be all right with you?"

"Yes," I said without thinking.

Later, I would tell myself that I invited him to talk, no other reason. I was delusional.

"Mommy will we go back to the cabinet now?" Allyson asked as we made our way to the restroom.

"Cabin, Allyson. And yes, I guess we could go back. Soon, anyway."

Robert was not there when I returned.

CHAPTER 24

Not wanting to return to the cabin too soon, I stayed in town as long as I could entertain Allyson. At Sticky Fingers, we treated ourselves. I had a cone of roasted sweet almonds, and Allyson devoured a cotton candy on a cone—the old-fashioned messy way.

"Mommy, let's go in here." Allyson's sticky fingers grabbed my arm.

A bright pink and purple gingerbread shop boasted windows filled with teddy bears and dolls complete with an old wooden train twisting in and out the toys. Sweet Annabelles was a child's delight, and miracles of miracles, there was the spitting image of Mary Jane just sitting on the back shelf waiting for Allyson—her pudgy little doll face framed by yellow pig tailed hair tied in red bows, the red polka dot dress, and shiny leather-looking Mary Jane shoes. Thank god Sweet Annabelles had a washroom for sticky fingers which we visited first. It saved the new Mary Jane.

"My Mary Jane. My Mary Jane. She's back from Oz, Mommy."

Standing in line to pay for our purchase, I thought I noticed the two young girls behind the counter point in our direction and giggle.

Were they laughing at us? Wow, was I getting paranoid? They were probably pointing at something else.

"Can we help you?"

Allyson held the new Mary Jane for dear life, and I searched for my wallet. The girls barely looked at me, no eye contact at all, almost as if embarrassed to look. They rang up the purchase price quickly, muttering a quick, "Thank you."

As I turned to leave, I thought I heard a muffled giggle again. I turned. The girls were huddled together, hands over mouths, clearly laughing. They were watching but looked quickly away. Another customer was ready to pay for a purchase. I was glad to leave the shop.

Before heading home, we stopped at the small supermarket in Hemlock Bay. Allyson rode in the cart as I picked up a few things for supper. I had paid with cash before, but being low on cash, I took out my checkbook. The clerk stared at my check and then at me.

"Is something wrong?" I asked.

"No." She put the check in the drawer and handed me the receipt.

Leaving the store, I saw that she was on the phone by her register. She gazed at me one last time and then turned quickly away to talk into the phone.

Was it my imagination? I packed my bags in the trunk, slamming the lid shut. If I hadn't overheard what I did at that coffee shop, I probably wouldn't have noticed anything else odd. My emotions were certainly getting the best of me. Or else this town was too weird to be true.

As I started the car, I thought I saw, just for a second, a person in my rearview mirror. She looked like the ghost on the pier, like the picture from the hope chest, and she stared right at me. I slammed on the brake; my heart was in my throat, but when I looked again, she was gone. Putting the car in park, I got out and walked around to the back just to make sure no one was there. No one was.

I felt tears well up in my eyes. I was so frustrated. Why was I being bothered like this? Were these ghosts real? Were they trying to direct me somewhere? Or was I just being delusional? Allyson was busy talking to her doll in the car. I was glad David was all but forgotten, and I had time to think. I probably shouldn't have said yes so quickly to Robert coming over tonight. He was getting too hard to keep resisting. What did I hope to gain by another encounter with him? I was married and going to stay married. It all felt so exciting, but was it worth it? We had a little history going now. I wanted a replay of our one romantic night and then again I didn't. Somehow resisting him now made me feel a bit better about myself. So why put temptation in my way? Then again, it was nearing the middle of August, and Jeb had made no effort to come up here. Every letter had made no effort to come up here. Every letter had an excuse. The thought reoccurred to me, could Jeb be having an affair? No, no. I put that thought out of my mind. Not Jeb, he was true blue. Starting a business was time-consuming. But that thought didn't make me feel a whole lot better. Jeb was good and working hard for us, and what was I doing?

"Mommy, are we almost there?"

Allyson's question broke into my thoughts.

"Almost, what should we do when we get back, sweetie? It's still warm enough to go swimming. Would you like that?"

"I want to play with David. Or fish."

"We'll fish!" Damn that David!

*****

I was so proud of myself. I called Robert. I didn't exactly talk to him, but I did leave a message. Had I actually been able to hear his voice and talk to him, things might have been different. I told him not to come. He was forgiven, and everything was fine. No need to come. I felt good at first, but then I felt lonely. That stupid indecision again. I thought of my mother-in-law being lonely and then finding a friend up here. What was her name? Chris? Kate? No, Karen. That was it, Karen. How nice to have a girlfriend to talk with. Lisa was almost but not quite like that. Bringing Lisa to mind didn't help any. I missed her fresh.

Early that evening, I made myself a strong vodka and tonic. I sat with Allyson on the edge of the pier drowning worms in Butternut Lake. There may have been plenty of fish in the pond, but none of them seemed to want to bite if Robert wasn't around. He never came and never returned my call. I was a bit disappointed, but then, it was better that way. I might have changed my mind.

"Mommy, David never got to fish." Allyson's simple statement broke into the silence and mingled with a lone motorboat in the distance.

I took a long, deep drink, finishing the contents of my glass.

"How come, Allyson? Why did David never get to fish? I mean, if you're going to live in the wall of our cabin, you should be able to fish."

"Well, he said he never got to fish."

I got up and pulled Allyson to her feet.

"Come with me, kiddo. I need to make another drink."

We walked together into the cabin. Allyson asked to stay outside but I said, "Absolutely not."

This drink contained less tonic, more vodka. I needed it tonight. We walked back to the pier. I felt slightly light-headed, even a bit giddy.

"So David never fished. He sits in the wall all day and waits for you to play."

Allyson ran ahead and grabbed her fishing pole, throwing the line in expertly. It made a quiet splash in the water. I thought she saw the worm fly off in the process, but why say anything? We weren't catching fish, anyway, and I didn't feel like touching another worm.

I gulped down the vodka.

CHAPTER 25

In the morning, I made a pot of coffee and tried to ease my conscience by writing Jeb a letter.

"Dear Jeb," I started and paused biting on the edge of my pen. What now? Should I say, "I want to inform you that I'm having an affair?" Well, maybe not really an affair. It was just once. Suddenly, I felt an immense sorrow. I was being totally selfish and unfair with Jeb. Unable to write, I put my pen on the bedside nightstand and drank my coffee. I was surprised I didn't have a headache this morning. I certainly had enough to drink last night. And a headache would have been a well-deserved penance.

Later that morning, riding into town again, I tried to put things into perspective. Did I love my husband? Yes, I did. Was I attracted to another man? Yes, I was. It was wrong. I knew it was wrong. But it felt so good, so right, so okay. Why? How would I feel if Jeb were to have an affair? Maybe he was. Did I care at this point? I wasn't too sure, and that was confusing.

The guilt, the guilt, it came in consuming waves. What should I do? My resolve to be decisive was ebbing.

I drove to the post office. I never did complete my letter to Jeb, but I wanted to check my box to see if I got any mail.

The post office was a busy place. All the vacationers of Hemlock Bay had to be there to check boxes or to mail packages. In a way, I was glad for the crowd. I wouldn't have to spend time answering the questions of the weird postmaster. I edged my way through the throng, holding onto Allyson's hand. Placing the silver key into my slot, I felt a stare. I should have been used to it by now. I often felt as if someone was following me or staring at me when I came to town. Then, I'd turn to see no one. It was a chilling feeling. But this time, I turned to see a pleasant older woman clad in tan shorts and pink rayon top, smiling at me.

"Good morning. Aren't you Mrs. Beinfield?"

Before I could answer she extended her hand. "I'm happy to meet you. My name is Karen."

CHAPTER 26

"How did you know who I was?" I stabbed at the ice cubes in my lemonade never taking my eyes off the congenial woman across from me. Karen smiled; soft wisps of silver white hair appeared to float across her forehead. The skin on her face was smooth and firm with a slight summer sun blush on her high cheekbones. Her eyes were tranquil blue, filled with wisdom—that is, if wisdom was discernable in eyes—and I think it was; her blue eyes seemed to have it. Karen removed the wrapper from her straw and inserted it into the glass watching it momentarily and then returning her dazzling smile to me.

"It feels as if it will be another hot day today. It's only morning, and already things are steamy."

She took a sip of her lemonade. Although her statement might have been a complaint of being too warm, her demeanor remained cool.

I could barely believe that I finally was meeting Karen. The Karen! I waited. She swallowed the liquid with the slowness and pleasure afforded those for whom time is no concern. I waited.

"I've been here about two weeks. I saw lights on in the Beinfield cottage."

"*Cottage.* I liked the sound of it, softer and easier sounding than *cabin.*"

She continued, "I asked around. I thought, maybe, the property had been sold. Some of my old friends in town pointed you out to me."

So some people in town actually did know who I was. Interesting.

"Mommy, I want more juice." Allyson had been quiet up to this point.

"Miss," Karen called to the passing waitress, "could you bring the child another glass of orange juice, please?" Then she smiled at Allyson. "Would you like something to eat, honey? A cookie? Some French fries?" She looked at me. "That is, if it's all right with your mother."

Allyson turned to me. "Can I have a cookie, Mommy? One of those kind with all that stuff on top."

"She means the frosted sugar cookies," I said to the waitress. "And yes, Allyson, you may have one."

"How old are you Allyson?"

Allyson held up three fingers.

"And how many is that?"

Karen started to count the fingers out loud as one does with a child, but Allyson blurted out, "I'm three. How many fingers are you?"

Karen laughed. "I'm more fingers than I have."

The waitress returned with the cookie and juice. Allyson busied herself licking the frosting. Normally, I would have insisted she take a bite, but today, I was happy that she stayed occupied for a while so I could converse.

"What was my mother-in-law like?"

The question had been burning inside me.

"Olivia and I were great friends and confidants."

I wondered if she knew everything? I could feel my heart pound with wild anticipation.

"We shared almost the same predicament, except my husband was nasty especially when he drank, which was almost all the time he was here. I was happy when he stayed in Chicago during the week. I dreaded weekends."

She took another leisurely swallow of her drink. I waited.

"It really is hot today. I don't remember it being so hot up here."

There it was again: a complaint of sorts yet her demeanor remained cool—a paradox.

Karen took yet another swallow of her lemonade, making me wait for my answer and then continued.

"Olivia, on the other hand, was sad—so very sad. I think she loved her Lester. I couldn't understand why he left her alone so much. I think Lester had problems—deep psychological ones. He'd be in counseling today, but forty years ago, well, one just muddled along. He was so jealous of Olivia. I swear he kept her up here thinking he was keeping her out of the eyes of other admirers. That's why he was so upset when he suspected a romantic entanglement."

Karen raised her eyebrows at this point, her eyes searching mine for some kind of reaction. I tried to remain calm so Karen would go on. It worked!

"But, of course," she continued, "it was his fault for leaving her alone so much. Olivia carried great guilt with her. One thing I can say for old Lester, he was nice to Olivia when he was here. Not like that old fart, I married." She laughed a high pitched but joyful laugh.

The laugh was contagious. I laughed. Allyson stopped her frosting licks long enough to giggle. It was also comical to hear this pristine and lovely woman refer to anyone as an old fart.

"Olivia went through some very trying times," she continued.

I became anxious, wondering if I would hear about Billy.

"She was a lovely woman. Even walking through town on Lester's arm, she turned heads. She had married so young that I don't believe she realized her potential or her hold on men."

Karen looked away as if involved in memory.

"My, she couldn't have been more than twenty when Lester left her up here by herself," she mumbled.

Her serene blue eyes took on a calming effect.

"And we didn't have the privilege of owning our own cars in those days. My only transportation, when the old fart was away, was a wooden rowboat." She laughed again.

"I remember rowing past Olivia's pier one day, and there she sat, crying her eyes out. I stopped to see if I could help, and that's how our friendship started."

"Did you see her often?" I asked to fill the quiet void when Karen stopped talking to finish her lemonade.

"Miss," Karen called to the waitress. "Might I have a glass of ice water, please? With plenty of ice!"

She turned back to me.

"Our cottages weren't very close. It was a long row. In the summer and fall, I'd row down about twice a week. On the weekends, I'd ask Harry (that was the first time she referred to her husband by name) to let me use the car, but he refused unless I offered to grocery shop. So I grocery shopped every Saturday that Les wasn't here, and I'd pick Olivia up."

"You mean he didn't come to the cabin every weekend?" I was surprised.

"No, he didn't. But I don't think it was because he didn't want to. I think that he was out of work much of the time and was job hunting in Milwaukee. He left Olivia up here partly because the cottage was paid for, and he couldn't afford another house in the city. I don't think he felt that he had to share this information with Olivia. You know how men were in those days."

She paused then patted my hand and continued.

"Well, maybe you don't know. Men felt that they had to be the breadwinners. They had to shoulder all the responsibilities. They had to be *men*. There wasn't as much give-and-take and sharing of roles as you see today."

Just as the waitress returned with the ice water, Allyson knocked over her juice.

"Your letter is getting soaked. You better pick it up," Karen warned.

I had taken one letter from my post office box. I had held it as we walked to the snack shop then carelessly put it on the table, not having looked at it due to my total involvement with Karen. We both grabbed some napkins to soak up the juice. I shook the liquid from the envelope and tucked the wet letter into my purse. The waitress returned with a towel to finish the cleaning. Little Allyson sat in anticipation of the punishment awaiting her.

"Accidents happen," I told her.

"Bring the child another juice," Karen told the waitress.

"How long was Olivia up here alone?" I asked as I gave my sopped napkins to the waitress.

"She was here about the same amount of time as I was, about four years. I think Lester got a job and bought a home in Milwaukee, and then he came for Olivia. By then, she had a child. What was really sad is Olivia didn't think that Lester believed the child to be his. I went back to Chicago and divorced Harry. And as luck would have it, he was killed about a month later in an auto accident."

The waitress returned with Allyson's juice. The child was now happily engaged in eating her cookie.

"Was there another baby before Jeffery?"

Karen looked toward Allyson and then raised her eyebrows in an effort to tell me that she didn't wish to talk about it with the child present.

"That child didn't make it," she whispered.

So Olivia did share all with her.

Karen continued, "Olivia and Lester may have used the cottage during the summers that followed. I don't know. We lost contact with each other. I thought about her often. She was so sad. She confided in me that she felt she was evil for things she had done and was beyond saving. She was such a nice person that I wanted to help her realize the Bible and the churches preached the ideal. But both preached forgiveness as well. Nobody lives up to the ideal all the time. Christians believe in the Savior who died for us and paid the price for sin. But Olivia couldn't buy that, and it caused her a lot of pain."

"There you are, Karen," a masculine voice broke into the conversation.

A tall white-haired gentleman towered over us. The top two buttons of his mint green shirt were opened, revealing wisps of gray chest hair. He gave the appearance of an athlete who still worked at keeping in shape. The summer sun had colored a blush on his broad face, and I couldn't help noticing his eyes—the same serene blue as Karen's. He grinned from ear to ear, looking every bit as pleasant as his partner.

Karen looked at her watch. "Oh my, it's past twelve. I'm so sorry, Roger. I'm not used to watching time." She turned her full attention to the man. "Roger, I'd like you to meet Stephanie Beinfield, Olivia's daughter-in-law."

"My pleasure." He extended a large sturdy hand with a firm grip.

"Roger is my husband," Karen explained. "We met long after the old Harry passed on. We had a luncheon date today at noon, and I'm afraid that I kept him waiting."

She started to rise, quite effortlessly, for what I considered to be her age.

"We're going to Wursel's for the best bratwurst in town. Would you and Allyson like to join us?"

I watched Allyson as she downed the remainder of her cookie with the rest of her juice.

"I don't think Allyson could take another hour in a restaurant. As much as I enjoy talking with you, I'm afraid we have to decline."

I rummaged in my purse for my wallet.

"Don't be silly." Karen grabbed the check the waitress had left on the table and handed it to Roger. "It's on me." She laughed again. "I mean on us." I nodded my head toward the smiling Roger.

"I'm really happy we met," I said to Karen as we made our way out into the bright sunshine.

She grabbed my hand, and I was startled to feel her cold flesh as she had just talked about being so hot. *It must be from holding onto the glass of iced water*, I thought.

"Trust in the Lord, and I know you will make all the right choices. I have a good feeling, right here." She put her hand on her heart.

"Thank you, Karen."

*****

To say she left me troubled would be an understatement. Karen had referred to me as Mrs. Beinfield until the end. And I don't ever remember telling her my first name. Did I mention it at the post office? I couldn't remember. She introduced me to Roger as Olivia's daughter-in-law. Did Roger even know Olivia? He came later in Karen's life. Unless she had talked to him about her past—that was a possibility, I guess. And what did she mean I would make all the right choices? I never mentioned I had choices to make. She did all the talking. Could she have gotten more information about me from her friends in town? And she acted as if she knew Olivia had died although she claimed to have lost track of her. It was perplexing.

CHAPTER 27

A day made in heaven! Allyson actually went down for a nap without too much resistance. It gave me a chance to bring out my lawn chair and soak up some rays without having to keep a watchful eye. As I sat in the sunlight, my mind wandered back to the afternoon I had sunbathed with Lisa. Tears welled up behind my eyelids. Was she happy in heaven? Did she know anything, see anything? I prayed letting the tepid sunlight warm my face. Thinking back this morning, meeting Karen, I liked her. She must have been a wonderful friend for Olivia. Suddenly, I thought about my letter. I jumped from the lawn chair and went in search of my purse. It was still on the kitchen table. Returning outside, I stared at the juice-stained envelope. It was from Jeb. Guilt pricked at my heartstrings when I read about his work schedule and all he had done this summer: work, get home late, a beer and a sandwich, a little TV, and then bed. But he was going to see it clear to come up north next week and possibly stay until I had to return home for school. It was good news. I think it was good news. It would keep me on the straight and narrow, wouldn't it? Is that what I wanted? Yes, of course it was what I wanted. I think. My mind drifted to the sensual moments with Robert. Did I really want to give that up? Where was my enchantment with him heading? Would I have to explain Robert to Jeb? How much do I tell him? Would he understand? Would I forever feel guilty living with a secret? My mind went back to my conversation with Karen.

"Olivia always felt so guilty. She couldn't accept that no one can live up to the ideal."

I wondered what made Karen so perceptive. Of course, faithfulness is the ideal. *How far from the ideal can I stumble*, I thought, *before there's no return?*

The heat of the noonday sun felt so comforting. Before long, my thoughts were just a blur mingling with the hum of boat motors on the lake and the far-off squeal of children enjoying the water. My mind drifted into a warming oblivion.

I didn't know if it was the ring of the cell phone or Allyson tugging at my arm that jarred me awake.

"Mommy, wake up."

I blinked an eye open as soft blond curls and an angelic face obstructed the glare of the sun. The hot, penetrating rays were angled, so half of my body was shaded by the tall pine tree behind me.

"Oh, honey, you're up." I yawned.

I managed to sit erect. The jingle of the cell phone pierced the air. "Do you know where mommy put the phone?"

Allyson put her small hands out as an offering; the cell phone was clutched in them.

"Thanks, honey."

"Hello?"

"Hi, there, Steph. Just wondering what the two of you are up to?"

"Hi, Robert. Actually, we both just woke from a nap."

"Must be nice," he answered. "Thought I might pop in about suppertime and see what you could cook up for us."

"Gosh, I-I don't know. I don't think I took anything out of the freezer."

Robert laughed. "The privilege of being on vacation. I'll bring some steaks. Do you think you could provide the rest?"

It was thrilling to hear from him. I wanted to tell him not to come. But I wanted him to come. Decisions are harder to make when one just wakes from a warm nap.

"I guess I could locate some edibles around here."

"Great. Tell Allyson I'll be over in the boat. We can fish after supper."

"Robert's coming for supper." I told my daughter. "Mommy has to see what kind of food we have."

"We got cookies and chips, Mommy."

I tousled her blond curls in much the same way as Robert always did. "That's great, hon. But I was thinking more in line with potatoes and veggies."

As I pulled out half a head of lettuce, two tomatoes, and an onion in the refrigerator and found a bag of salad potatoes, a stalk of celery, and a jar partially filled with mayo, I half regretted my answer to Robert. Jeb would be coming next week. That would be the end of this Robert thing. What if Allyson said something? We were friends, just friends. Obviously, my prayer didn't work. Where was my self-control? Oh well, we're just having supper. Allyson is with us. I'll ask him to leave by evening. Yes, that's what I'll do. Then again, maybe I won't. I've already fallen from grace, so to speak; why not one more time? The idea excited me. It felt like champagne bubbles cursing through my veins. Then when Jeb comes, if he comes, I'll make my decision then.

Setting a pot of water to boil, I gazed at the kitchen clock. It was half past three. There was time to make the potato salad and have it cool. I fixed Allyson a slice of bread spread thick with peanut butter and sent her into her bedroom to play.

"But I want to swim," she protested.

"After I get the potato salad made, we'll have time for a swim. Go and give your dolls some lunch. It'll just be a little while." Then as an afterthought, "Robert is bringing his boat. We'll go fishing later."

I felt a bit lightheaded from my nap in the sun. My face pinched with a slight burn. Standing at the sink, I splashed some cool water on my blushed complexion. It felt refreshing but my face still pinched. I walked into the bathroom to get my cream. Where did I put it? I shook my head in an effort to clear out some of the drowsiness then remembered. On "clean up, fix up" day, I put creams and things in the cabinet under the sink. I sat on the bathroom floor, on the cool scrubbed linoleum and rummaged through the under-the-sink cabinet. As I moved jars and bottles aside looking for my tube of after-sun lotion, I saw a peeling edge of contact paper near the corner of the shelf. Tearing a large chuck with one hand as I grabbed my tube of lotion, I mused, here I go again. I had thought that all the messages written had been discovered by now. Olivia had been one busy person. The under cabinet wood was wavy and peeled due to years of water damage. I guess that's why it was covered with the plastic sheet. Surprisingly, the message wasn't too difficult to decipher. Large chunks of letters were missing, but I was able to manage to get their meaning.

No one knows how l nely and sad I fee. Life
is e bing away from me, piece by piece.
That which is taking my life, is growing inside of me.
Growing like a weed
I am being punished
If only my life could serve some purpose.
help someone to benefit from my errors.
Olivia Sept. 1981

Apparently, this message was written on a visit to the cabin after Olivia had been diagnosed with cancer. It was so forlorn, yet it contained a glimmer of hope that somehow her mistakes might help someone else.

So you think you're helping me, Olivia? Your messages are confusing. Are you telling me to forget Jeb and make sure I don't lose Robert? Or are you telling me to be faithful to your son? You are one damn confusing woman. Here I go again, letting a ghost help me make my decisions. Damn. When would I ever learn? I'm forty. Way past time to make my own choices. I was a bit angry with myself. I replaced the torn contact paper with a towel in an effort to hide the writing and cover the destroyed wood. I didn't feel like dealing with it at the moment. My jars of creams on top would hold it in place. Surprisingly, I no longer felt foolish communicating with ghosts. It had become an everyday affair.

Determined not to ruin this perfectly, lovely summer day, I spent the rest of the afternoon enjoying the great outdoors with my daughter. We came in about six to a ringing cell phone vibrating on the kitchen table.

"Hi, Steph, where were you? This thing has been ringing forever."

"Hi, Robert, Allyson and I were in the lake. I forgot to take the phone with me. Sorry."

"I'm glad you were enjoying the day. I, on the other hand, am having a trying time. Things have gotten hectic around here. I won't be able to make it tonight. Will you take a rain check for tomorrow?"

I felt a pang of disappointment, but it was possibly my salvation. I had another chance at self-control, but I didn't quite know how to word my response. Robert had been nothing but nice. I didn't want to ruin things.

"Steph, are you still there?"

I hadn't realized I was taking so long to answer.

"Umm, yes, I'm here."

"Rain check tomorrow then?"

"Umm, we might be busy."

"Busy, you say?"

"Jeb's coming next week."

"I'm not asking about next week. Tomorrow. See you tomorrow."

Click. We were disconnected.

I didn't have to exercise self-control this time. I could do it tomorrow.

CHAPTER 28

That evening, Allyson and I sat at the picnic table dining on potato salad. There was one thing I was happy about. Allyson hadn't mentioned David all day. Of course, that silence was spoiled during her night prayers when she stated, "And God bless David. I'm going to teach him to fish."

After Allyson fell asleep, I searched my kitchen cupboards for a bottle of cranberry wine which the North was famous for producing.

"If you come up here in the fall, we could visit the cranberry bogs about the time the berries are harvested," Robert had told me the day we had visited the winery in town.

He bought me three bottles of the wine along with a carton of cold pack cheddar cheese laced with the deep red liquid.

Balancing the bottle, a stemmed glass, and a paper plate loaded with crackers and cheese, I went to sit on the pier to enjoy the early evening in solitude. The bottle popped easily, and the sloshing sound of the wine pouring into my glass mingled with the sound of the gentle brown waves of Butternut Lake washing along the shore. The purple evening sky was ablaze with the promise of millions of twinkling stars. It was a warm night made comfortable by a gentle summer breeze. The sweet wine created a tingling path from the tip of my tongue to the pit of my stomach. A pontoon boat filled with people laughing, drinking, and having a good time floated down the middle of the lake. Suddenly, I felt lonely as I watched the large boat disappear around a bend. A young couple in a canoe slipped by the front of my pier so close I could almost touch them. They had been so quiet I did not hear them coming.

"Hi." They waved to me, smiling.

Their paddles dipped into the water and moved them along silently.

It must have been like that the day Karen rowed by the first time, I thought. Then again, an old rowboat with oars would have made more noise. But if Olivia was busy crying, she probably didn't hear Karen coming.

I sat on the edge of the pier, legs dangling in the cool brown water and gazed in both directions as well as across the lake, wondering in which direction was Karen's cabin. We had never discussed where it was located, only that it had been a long row. The shoreline was dotted with small and large homes, some old, some new. Many of them were occupied only on weekends. Some were always vacant, their piers old and tumbling, tall grass growing around them surrounded only by memories. As darkness overtook the sky, the stillness brought an inner peace. The wine worked as a barrier against the loneliness that plagued me. I poured and drank, poured and drank. Suddenly, only an inch of darkness was left near the bottom of the bottle.

"Boy, am I going to have a headache," I murmured to myself. "I don't remember drinking all of this."

Not wanting to ruin tomorrow, if that was still possible, I turned the bottle over and let the rest of the red liquid mix with the dark water of Butternut Lake. It made a gentle splash.

"Here, fishy, fishy, have a drink on me." I giggled at my private joke and slipping into my sandals, weaved my way back to the cabin just as the first mosquito of the evening took a delicious bite of my arm. I slapped at it sending the empty wine bottle reeling out to sea.

Oops.

I watched it float on the small waves until it came back to shore.

I walked in the wet sand, sinking in my sandals to capture my bottle, pulling it from its watery grave. I almost lost my balance.

I didn't think cranberry wine carried such a punch. I giggled to myself.

I'll never forget that night. As I remember it now, it was a turning point in my life, for sure. Sleep came easily. Maybe it was the wine. Then the dreams started. Maybe that was the wine also. Karen was in my cabin, and I was showing her Olivia's messages. Then, suddenly, I became Olivia, and I was showing the freshly written messages to Karen. I felt so sad I cried. Karen held my hand and said soft things, although I couldn't make out the words, just the sounds. Next, there was the bright light in the sky—an explosion. It was like a rerun of an old movie. I saw this one before. I ran to the bedroom window, and there was Allyson and Lisa standing on the pier again, their backs to the cabin. I was surprised and delighted to see Lisa was back, but my joy only lasted a second. The ball of fire sent out streaks in all directions, and the longest streak stretched to the children.

Run. I tried to yell. Run back in here. But my words choked on my breath. Everything turned blinding white. Then it was dark again, so dark. I could hardly make out the pier, but I knew that no one was standing there. The children were gone, consumed by the fire. There was a bang, like a door slamming. Someone came in. I thought. But who? Did the children come back? Were they saved? My heart felt a rush of hope. Then the darkness and dread settled over the feeling, pushing it out. Was the bang the intruders? Did they get in this time? I woke with a start.

My head pounded miserably as I made my way into the dark of the kitchen. Everything was quiet. But the door was ajar.

Funny, I thought I closed and locked it; I pulled it shut.

On my way back to bed, I opened the door of Allyson's room to check on my sleeping daughter. But the bed was empty. I turned on the light to be sure. It was empty.

"Allyson?" I walked into the kitchen.

Allyson was nowhere in the cabin.

"Shit. Allyson!"

I turned on the porch light and opened the door. I yelled her name into the blackness. I panicked. Did I hear the door bang for real? Did Allyson open it and leave? But it was so dark; she wouldn't do that by herself, would she? Did I forget to lock the door? Damn. Why did I drink so much wine? I don't remember.

I made my way down to the pier stumbling over a stone then a root as my walk broke into a run. The pier was empty as it had been at the end of my dream.

"Allyson" I called. But I could not see in the darkness.

Why hadn't I brought a flashlight? I ran back to the cabin for a flashlight and then remembered the cell phone on the kitchen table. What I needed was help!

It rang a number of times.

"Robert, answer, damn it." I pleaded.

Finally, on the fifth ring a sleepy voice said, "Hello?"

"She's gone, Robert. She's gone."

"What?" The voice on the other end sounded more alert. "Who's gone?"

"Allyson." I cried into the phone. "I went in her room, and she's not there."

"Hold on a minute, Steph. Look again."

"She's not there." This time I yelled.

"Look under the bed and all over. *Now.*"

I ran into the bedrooms and did as Robert said. I returned breathless.

"Now will you believe me? She's not here, Robert."

"I'll be right over. Look outside, but stay near the cabin. Check the shore."

I ran out in my night clothes again. Maybe I overlooked some obscure area.

"Allyson, Allyson." I called as I walked around the cabin and then to the entrance of the forest where Allyson had walked the last time she was missing. The trees formed a ghostly tunnel, and I felt leery of entering this forbidden void. Surely, a small child would not brave a walk in there. I stood at the entrance calling my daughter's name.

"Oh, dear God," I prayed, "help me find her. Let her be all right."

Lights flashed as Robert's car pulled up to the side of the cabin. I ran to meet him.

"Robert, I can't find her."

"We'll find her."

He took his flashlight and headed down to the pier. I followed him. He threw the beam of light up and down the shoreline.

He leaped off the pier and sloshed in the shallow water along the shore, returning with a small bundle in his arms. Putting the child down, he proceeded giving mouth to mouth, turning her on her side and bringing her arms over her head. He breathed a sigh of relief as lake water spurted from the corners of her mouth.

I froze with his cell phone in my hand.

"She's alive. She must not have been in the water all the while we were looking for her. For god's sake, Steph, dial 911!"

We had Allyson in the car and met the ambulance on the road. Transferring into the white vehicle, the paramedics took over. Allyson was rushed to the hospital in Minnow Point. I remember sitting in the waiting room in a gray sweatshirt and a pair of jeans thrown carelessly over my nightshirt. Robert waited with me.

"I never heard her leave the house except maybe in a dream." I wailed.

"She had a fishing pole in her hand when I found her," Robert said. "What would possess her to go out fishing at night?"

He held me, and I remember sobbing in his arms.

"Mrs. Beinfield."

I turned to face the young doctor, scared to death at what I would hear.

"She took quite a bit of water into her lungs, but we think most of it is out. She hasn't regained consciousness yet, so we need to keep a close watch. The next few hours will be very critical, but we think she will make it."

"Oh, thank God. Do you really think she'll be all right?"

The doctor shook his head affirmatively but said, "I hope so."

Robert put his arm around me again. "You know, you really should call Jeb."

I dialed home but got my answering machine at first.

"Hi, who is this?" Jeb's voice broke in, cutting the tape.

"Jeb, there's been an accident." I didn't take a breath to give him a chance for a reply; I continued in a rush. "We found Allyson in the lake, but the doctors think she'll be okay. We're in the hospital in Minnow Point. Allyson is still unconscious." I chocked on my last sentence.

Jeb, if shocked, sounded more in control than I felt.

"I'll drive up there." He paused, possibly to gaze at the bedside clock. "I'll meet you at the hospital about six."

During the next four hours, Robert sat with me, bringing me black, hot coffee, speaking in soft tones. I even remember him praying with me. At least I think he was there praying with me.

"No change," the nurses said when I walked to her room.

Her little body was buried under the white hospital sheets connected to hoses dripping in her arm. I touched her little arm, the one that wasn't connected to anything. I brushed the soft, damp curls from her forehead.

"Please, God, please," I prayed, "let her live. I'll change. I'll do what's right. I promise. Just let her live."

"Allyson," I whispered in my child's ear, "Mommy's here. I love you. Please come back."

I did not know when Robert left my side, and Jeb took his place. I had no idea if the two met. Soft sunlight swam into the hospital window bathing the room in the cheery light of day. Jeb was at my side when Allyson's eyelids flickered. It was a good sign.

"She'll be fine," The morning nurse smiled and left the room.

"Mommy, Daddy." Allyson looked at us.

"We're here, honey."

"David said when I wake up, Mommy and Daddy would be here."

"Who's David?" Jeb asked.

Before I could answer, Allyson replied, "He's my friend, and I taught him how to fish."

Jeb and I stayed at the hospital all day and into the evening. Allyson sat up and ate with us. The doctors wanted her to stay one more night, just to be sure everything was all right. I wouldn't leave her side until she was asleep for the night. We drove back to the cabin in silence, both feeling relieved and tired. By the time we arrived, I was drained emotionally and in no mood for conversation.

So when Jeb said, "I'll make us some coffee; we need to talk."

I resounded with an emphatic, "No, not now."

Having second thoughts about my outburst caused me to grope for an explanation for my sudden negative answer.

"I'm exhausted. We can talk tomorrow. We have to be at the hospital in the morning. We can talk on the way there."

I remember not wanting to discuss Robert if that was what was bothering him.

"Okay, hon. Tomorrow is fine. I love you."

I looked at Jeb. His face appeared more masculine to me, if not a bit older. His eyes were so turquoise. Funny, I didn't remember them being so turquoise. Deep blue tending toward green when tired or angry, yes, but never turquoise. It was attractive. Maybe it was the dim light in the cabin kitchen or the drowsiness in my eyes. But it looked good on him. I liked it. His hair lay in dark waves, and a becoming shadow graced his face. It didn't look shaggy to me this time; it looked masculine and even a bit sexy. I reached up and touched the face I had loved in a time before all this. It was warm and rough. Could his face block out the memory of Robert? I felt a stir of tenderness toward him. *I have to give him a chance*, I thought.

Jeb took my gesture as an affirmative answer. He smiled weakly and touched my face in return. I swallowed my fears. He deserved some explanations.

"It's all right, Jeb. We can talk for a minute."

He rose and brought us coffee.

I felt "coffee-ed out." I complained, but I accepted the warm cup. Wrapping my hands around it, I let the steam melt my face. Then I took a comforting sip. To my amazement and relief, the only thing he inquired about is how I thought Allyson got out of the cabin and why she left? I answered his questions to the best of my ability and then decided to ask him some of my own.

"Do you remember living in this cabin?"

"I really don't remember much. I think I was about two or three when my mother and I moved back to Milwaukee. We spent a few summer's here after that. It's just a feeling I remember—a feeling of loneliness and despair. My mother was so unhappy, and I think it wore off on me, being an only child."

"Jeb, do you know why your mother was so unhappy?"

He leaned back in his chair. "I know she hated being stuck up here in the winter. I know my dad was gone a lot and not very affectionate when he was around. Kind of like I've been with you, being so involved with the business and all. I'm really sorry, hon."

His realization came as an unexpected but appreciated shock to me.

"I'm not really sure my mother planned on having me. I know my father didn't."

"What makes you say that?"

"I don't feel that I was unloved, but I have the distinct feeling that I was unwanted or at least unexpected."

We sat in silence for a short time, each gathering thoughts.

"Lisa told me that you and Sara stayed here."

"That's right. We did. Once."

"Did either of you ever read any of your mother's messages?"

"Messages?" Jeb raised an eyebrow.

Clearly, he didn't have a clue.

"You mentioned something like that in one of your letters. I really didn't know what you were talking about."

I headed for the cereal cabinet, removing all of the boxes some of which fell to the floor in my haste. My efforts revealed some scratches in the wood, nothing clearly readable.

"I don't believe it. Honestly, something was written here. Both Lisa and I saw it. This was the first message we read."

Jeb was as confused as I, but he rose and put both of his arms around me, a gentle bear hug. It felt so comforting.

"You've had a trying day. Settle down, hon."

I wiggled out of his grasp and ran to the bathroom.

"They were here. They were all here. I saw them. Lisa saw them."

Jeb followed me into the bathroom. Surely, the last message I read had to be there under the towel. I pulled the toiletries out, and they softly clanked as they fell to the floor. Lifting the towel, I revealed the wavy pealing wood with marks, but nothing readable as a message.

"I don't understand this." I looked at Jeb. "They were here. Clear as day."

I stood to face my husband. "There were more." I pushed at him making my way out of the bathroom. I was a crazed woman. He followed, and we looked in all the places. Each spot showed scratches of some type, but none contained a readable message. I ran into my bedroom and took the bottom drawer from the dresser emptying the clothes on my bed. I moved the honey maple dresser and looked behind the mirror. Nothing. In despair and disbelief, I sat on the edge of the bed absentmindedly moving my clothes aside.

"This is like a nightmare," I said covering my face for a moment. Then I looked into Jeb's tender eyes as mine filled with tears of frustration. "You don't believe me, do you? You think I'm nuts."

Jeb sat down next to me gently moving some clothes aside. "I believe that this cabin is weird. There are secrets here, and those secrets were the base of my childhood problems."

He put his arms around me. "It doesn't matter. It doesn't matter what you say you read here. I believe you. You have had a very trying day. It makes for a lot of confusion."

But I had a difficult time letting it go at that. My relief in not having to explain Robert, at least not this time, was lost in my bewilderment.

"Jeb, did your mother have a friend up here named Karen?"

Jeb shook his head affirmatively. "Yes, she did. Of course, I don't remember her, but I remember my mother talking about her."

At last! I thought hopefully. At last, we'll make some sense of all of this!

"I met Karen yesterday, in town. We talked."

Jeb jumped off the side of the bed as if he were stung. "You can't be serious."

"I'm very serious. Allyson was with me."

He leaned against the dresser across from the bed, holding the edge to steady himself.

"You couldn't have met Karen yesterday. It wasn't Karen."

"I did meet her," I insisted, "at the post office. We went to the coffee shop, and I met her husband Roger there. We talked over an hour. She told me about your mother."

"You couldn't have met Karen or Roger."

Jeb leaned over and put his hands on my shoulders grabbing hard for emphasis. "Karen and Roger moved to California. Remember that earthquake they had out there a few years back? The one where the freeway bridge collapsed?"

I shook my head affirmatively, wondering what he was getting at.

"They were driving on that bridge. They were both killed."

Fresh fear and bewilderment bubbled up and filled my head.

Jeb straightened his bulky frame, putting both hands on the dresser behind him leaning back. He looked thoughtful.

"Maybe I'm wrong," he ventured. "I don't remember if I read about them or if someone told me about them. I could be mistaken."

"Thank you, Jeb. At least I only feel half nuts."

He embraced me. He felt warm and reassuring. The excitement I felt with Robert was not there, but something deeper, something so steady and good welled up inside of me. It was just what I needed at the moment. It was relaxing.

"Honey, I haven't been the best of husbands. I've been so preoccupied with the business that I've forgotten my family needs to come first. I'm so sorry. Things are going to change."

I didn't know if that was just supposed to be a comforting thing you say to a crazy person to calm her down or if he really meant it, crazy wife or not. I didn't care. It was comforting to be in his arms, to have him care, to feel loved. I'd figure it all out later. Now I just wanted peace.

CHAPTER 29

We drove back to the hospital the next morning, to pick up Allyson, passing through Hemlock Bay. I stared at the fire and police station and saw Robert's car in the parking lot.

Jeb never asked about Robert. And I'll never say anything. Why should I? It was all a dream, all part of the mystic of this summer. It's over. My heart skipped a beat as I gazed at Hemlock Bay slipping away in the side view mirror of the car. This is for the best. Life in this northern town is drawing to a close. It dawned on me that maybe these past two horrid days were God's way of answering my prayer and putting an end to something that was not right. *But what if Allyson says something?* I thought in a panic. Well, I'd have to handle that at the time. I'd pray for guidance this time before doing anything rash. Jeb would just have to deal with the information. If he truly loved us, he would learn to forgive and forget. If he didn't forgive, then oh well, I would have to deal with that too. It would be awful, but I have to give Jeb that chance. I planned to forgive myself also and start over. I gazed at Jeb who looked at me and took my gaze as a look of affection. He smiled before looking back to the road. Jeb never said anything about him having an affair while I was gone. But why would he? Maybe he had secrets too. Since I had my secret, I was not going there. If he ever shared something like that with me, I'd come out in the open also. Then we both could forgive. Sometimes secrets aren't meant to share. There are times when these things should be kept private and forgotten. From this day forward, we could be honest with each other and true to our marriage. It would work. With the help of God, I'd make it work.

Allyson was happy to see us. We decided not to return to the cabin. We could be home in Milwaukee by four in the afternoon. The next weekend, we would leave Allyson with my mother and come back to gather my things. Maybe we'd spend a few days alone enjoying the lake.

I guess I accomplished my goal of coming north. At least it was seeming that way. Jeb acted as if he realized his family needed more attention. The business was still going to take a lot of his time, but he was willing to try harder to make time for us. And me? I realized that I had to cut him some flack. He needed to work long hours to succeed for us. I would have to work with him to plan special occasions and times for romance. I had to realize that as our children (and we would have more) grew older, we would have extra time for the two of us. I needed to be patient. I needed to be more loving myself. Together, we would make it work. This crazy woman was going home. Summer was over. My first affair was over. My delusion was over. The messages were gone. Were they ever there? I had thought those messages and Olivia's spirit were directing my life. How could I have been so stupid? I'm directing my life from now on. It was the end of the summer and time to return home, anyway. The end of a dream.

CHAPTER 30

It was all so strange, Allyson never mentioned David again. A few days after we had come home, Jeb asked her who David was. Allyson looked at him strangely as if she did not understand the question. I wondered. All those messages. The ghosts. David. Even Karen. Were they real? If they were real, were they good or bad? Allyson was with me when I was with Karen, but how could I be validated by a three year old? Was I being led to make mistakes? Or was I being forced to realize that I was strong and wise enough to make my own decisions, with God's help, of course? Maybe I was just delusional. Oh well, what does it matter? It's over. Done. I'm free.

The death of Lisa, disappearing messages and ghosts, the strangeness of it all was dark when I thought of it. I wasn't interested in keeping the cabin neither was Jeb. We could use the money in its sale and travel when we had the time. We both agreed on this.

The weekend Jeb and I returned to empty the cabin of personal items and list it with the realtor, I remembered that I had never thanked Robert for all he had done after Allyson's accident. Anyway, it was a way to see him again, to put closure to things. I was curious and frightened about my feelings.

"I have to go into town," I told Jeb as we were packing things in the kitchen. "There's someone I have to thank. Someone who saved Allyson's life."

"I'll come with you," Jeb volunteered.

"No, I have to do this alone."

If Jeb was disturbed by my answer, he didn't show it. "That's fine, hon. I'll continue to pack things while you're gone."

I sure hope I'm doing the right thing, I thought as I drove into town. Help me, Jesus. I have to say the correct things. I have to feel the correct feelings. I had stopped being a praying person. I got caught up in the reality of life, so my feelings and frequent praying now surprised even me. It was the middle of September. The sumac on the side of the road was brilliant scarlet. Gold and orange Indian paint brushes had replaced the wild daisies. Nature had begun painting some of the leaves brilliant yellow; a few were turning red while hardier green leaves were hanging on to their color for just a moment longer. A chill nipped the air.

The past two weeks with Jeb had been fine. I didn't want to rekindle anything with Robert. And yet…I had this need, this real need to see him again and to put closure to this strange summer. And, yes, I did have to thank him. I couldn't just leave. It wouldn't be right. I was making excuses to see Robert again. I knew that. But somehow, I knew I had to do it. I couldn't go on without this finality. But what if the feelings would stir? Would I really be able to leave Robert and return to Jeb? Somehow, I was driven. I had to find out. But this time, I prayed for guidance.

*****

I was glad that Robert's car was in the parking lot. I was greeted by a woman in blue uniform behind a counter by the front door.

"I'd like to see Mr. Tucker."

"He's on the phone right now. Would you care to wait? Or is this an emergency?"

"It's no emergency. I'll wait."

I gazed around the small reception room, the starkness of its plain white walls broken with framed photographs of Hemlock Bay. Four empty chairs separated by a round lamp table were along the far wall.

"Who can I say is calling?" The receptionist asked.

"Tell him it's Stephanie."

When I was ushered into his office ten minutes later, he rose to greet me—a bright smile on his face. For the first time, I noticed lines of wrinkles about his eyes and mouth. It made him appear older. I also noticed a coffee stain on his otherwise spotless blue shirt—a sign of imperfection. I felt uncomfortable at noticing trifle things about the man who had meant so much to me—a man I had been intimate with and the man who had saved Allyson's life.

He did not move to embrace me but rather motioned for me to be seated. I wondered if he suspected the reason for my visit.

"I came to thank you for everything. You've been great to us."

"It was my pleasure. I called the hospital several times to see how she was. I decided against contacting you since the hospital staff told me your husband was with you."

"That was thoughtful."

There was a moment of awkward silence; an icy stillness permeated the room. During this moment, I couldn't decide how I felt about him. His root beer eyes that had been so intoxicating had lost their sparkle. It had been the sparkle, not the color that I was infatuated with.

"We're selling the cabin," I felt compelled to continue, my voice sounding flat and lifeless. "Jeb is there now packing personal things that we'll be taking home."

I paused, but he said nothing. I remember us looking at each other, and the gaze was painful. With a heavy heart, I continued.

"I guess I also came to say goodbye."

Robert's smile faded. He continued to stare at me thoughtfully.

"Are you happy, Steph? I mean is everything all right with you?"

I noticed that he did not mention Jeb.

"Everything is fine and, yes, I guess I'm as happy as I ought to be."

"Are you sure?"

"I'm pretty sure. Only time will tell."

"Then I'm happy for you. I'll always be here in case you change your mind."

He stood as if to end the conversation. It was a shock to me that he took everything so calmly and seemingly wanted this show to end quickly. Yet his demeanor had changed since I first walked into his office. He seemed disappointed; yes, that was the word: *disappointed.*

Did he actually say *I'll always be here in case you change your mind?* Or did I just imagine that he said it? It seemed to be the right thing to say, the thing they say in movies, so did I just think I heard that? What did it matter? I stood and not knowing what to do next, I extended my hand.

"Thank you so much, Robert, for everything. If it wasn't for you, Allyson might, might—" I chocked and couldn't continue.

He bypassed my hand and took me in his arms kissing the top of my head. *I know he said he'd always be here,* I thought. This proves it. He did say it. It gave me a warm feeling holding his body close to mine, sending tingles of excitement up my spine, but I willed them away. He released me quickly and looked into my eyes, his hands on my shoulders. I moved my face slightly to the side to avert any contact for fear my reserve would fail me. He seemed not to notice.

"If ever you have a change of heart, you know where to find me," he whispered.

I could feel my eyes well with tears. It was like the end of an era, the finish of a story. I swallowed the lump in my throat willing myself not to cry and looked back at Robert.

"Thank you, Robert. I will. I promise."

That afternoon, Jeb and I went to see the real estate agent.

*****

We didn't return to Hemlock Bay until the middle of October to sign papers. The cabin had a buyer. The woods were livid with crimson and maroon and glowing oranges and golds. The sun seemed brighter, illuminating the entire forest road, turning everything golden. Nature had painted a picture to behold. Some of the trees had prematurely lost their leaves, and they stood naked in the woods. The forest floor was littered with purple and brown foliage. A few piers remained in the water, the die-hards. Most were upside down along the lakefront looking like broken bridges. It was a different feeling—exhilarating, fresh but sad like an ending.

I'd love to share the fall with you. It's beautiful up here with all the colors, was what Robert had said eons ago. I banished the thought from my mind.

"You know," Jeb interjected. "We'll have the money now to buy a time-share in Jamaica or maybe a condo in Florida."

"I think I would like that, either one," I answered absentmindedly. "We'll look into it."

CHAPTER 31

The O'Conners seemed like a pleasant couple. They were so excited about buying their "up north cabin" as they called it. Chuck O'Conner was robust with an easy laugh and brilliant auburn hair. His young wife, Ginger, reminded me of a doll I once owned—a Ginny doll, the Barbie doll predecessor. Ginger's hair fell in soft brown ringlets around her simply pretty and innocent-looking face. They were a young and enthusiastic couple. I couldn't help wondering where they found the money to buy a summer home. They were dressed in jeans and matching gray sweat shirts. They had arrived in a small black truck and didn't seem to be the type to be oozing spare money. But the bank had granted them a loan, and here they were, ready to buy. I hoped they would find peace and happiness in the Northwoods.

I requested one last look in the cabin before signing the papers. I wanted to make sure that none of the messages were visible. They weren't. Strange. Maybe it was my imagination all along. There were the scratches, but even they appeared lighter, and they said nothing. Of course, Lisa wasn't here to validate anything either.

Olivia was just talking to me. I was sure of it now. Here I go, reverting to ghost talk again. It was my interpretation of a dead woman's writing. Olivia wasn't telling me anything. Maybe, just maybe, I possessed the wisdom and ability to come to grips with reality and make my own decisions. Whatever, I was willing to accept life as it was and the love for my little family was complete.

Driving home, through Hemlock Bay, Robert's police car passed us. He didn't notice me, but I couldn't mistake the blond hair and the fading tanned profile. I gazed at him, and my heart gave a leap.

Willing the commotion within me to cease, I turned to concentrate, instead, on Jeb's profile. There were two men in my life. And I loved them both in different ways. Robert was fresh, exciting, and fun to be with. Jeb had been comforting and steady, and he was fun to be with when love was new, and I trust we'll have good times together again. I watched Jeb as he drove. My future was with him. I was sure of that now. I was so happy that he never asked any probing questions about the summer. I was determined to rekindle the spark, to work at the marriage. I settled back against the car seat feeling very content, at least for this moment.

"Thank you for Olivia and for David and especially for Karen, even if they were figments of my imagination." In a strange way, they had helped me find the strength within me to make good decisions—decisions I made. It seemed as if God had placed them in my life.

CHAPTER 32

The Discovery, June 1997

The weather was too nice to be working indoors. Ginger looked longingly at the lake where the whole world seemed to be at play. A jet skier sent a rooster spray high into the warm air. The breeze carried the squeal of children splashing in the water.

Up until today, the young summer had been cool and damp. It wasn't difficult to spend it renovating a newly purchased cabin. Ginger remembered the cool October day she and Chuck signed the papers making the cabin theirs. It had been "love at first sight" viewing the chocolate brown hewed logs of the small dwelling facing Butternut Lake. Ginger appreciated the way the water's reflection danced on the walls and ceiling inside the cabin. Chuck decided to finish the kitchen/living room walls with the wood panels.

"Hey, helper!"

She was called back to reality.

"I need your assistance. This was partly your idea, you remember."

"I'm coming, slave driver."

Inside the cabin, Chuck was in the middle of a mess. He couldn't put wood over papered clapboard, no, not Chuck.

"Something worth doing is worth doing well," he said.

He was removing the inner walls to check the wiring before insulation. Down came the kitchen cabinets, Chuck would build new. Ginger surveyed the mess of renovation.

"Do you think we need to do all of this, Chuck? I mean, do you think we'll ever be here in the winter?"

"Come here. I need you to grab the edge of this board as I take it down," Chuck answered.

Ginger moved in to help. When Chuck was involved, he was totally involved. He had selective hearing. Ginger grabbed the long clapboard sheet, its underside in her view.

"Hey, Chuck, look at this. Chuck!"

The flaming red head of Charles Allen O'Conner peered around the sheet.

"What?"

"There's a note painted on this board. Look! It says, 'Built with love on a sunny May Day Olivia and Lester 1951.'"

Chuck moved his head at an angle to survey the underside of the board.

Ginger was nostalgic. "We need to save this."

Chuck was anything but. "Pretty cool, hon. But what would we do with it? Put it on the burn pile."

"You know what's wrong with you, Chuck?" Ginger kept the conversation going as she helped to carry the wood outdoors.

"I give. What's wrong with your husband this time?"

"You have no imagination."

They struggled to get the wood sheet out the door.

"All right, Picasso." Beads of sweat glistened on Chuck's brow as he tried another angle to get it through the door.

"You figure out a way to make that note a smaller work of art, and we'll give it a place of distinction."

The wood was set against the side of the cabin.

"You're on." Ginger was already toying with some ideas.

"I might need your help again soon. Chuck warned as he turned to go back inside.

"Do you think we could enjoy the day a little? It's the first we had sun in weeks," Ginger implored.

Chuck gazed at his watch before disappearing inside. "Let's give it another three hours," he called into the air. "Four o'clock will be a good time for a swim."

Ginger remained fairly content staying out in the sunshine picking up pieces of clapboard and wood, throwing them into the firepit. The loose nails and other metal were put in a rusty coffee can. Occasionally, she walked back to the piece of clapboard leaning against the cabin.

"*Built with love,*" she read over and over again. *How romantic,* she thought. I wonder who Lester and Olivia were?

"Hey, Ginger, I need you."

Chuck's yell came from within the cabin. Ginger found him lifting sheets of clapboard from the wall facing the road where the kitchen cabinets had been. It opened into the lean-to structure that housed the hot water heater, but it opened a much larger space.

"I wondered why that structure looked so much bigger from the outside," Chuck said. "There's another small room on this side."

Planks had been haphazardly nailed across the opening over which the clapboard had been nailed.

"It looks like it was a closet or pantry or something," Ginger added.

She surveyed the interior. There were still some shelves nailed to the sidewalls. It was just large enough for both of them to work side by side. Ginger helped to remove the shelves.

"It looks as if something is written on this wall."

Ginger brought a flashlight for a better look. Its watery beam illuminated writing, but it was not discernible. Using a wedge, Chuck wiggled the wallboard free.

"There's something behind here."

Ginger's flashlight reflected back from a metal container buried in the wall. Together they lifted a green metal toolbox from its hiding place and placed it on the kitchen floor.

"Why would anyone bury a toolbox?"

A toolbox was one of life's necessities to Chuck. Burying one in a wall was unthinkable. Chuck gave the box a shake, and they felt, more than heard, the thud.

"Feels like one big tool inside."

Ginger wiped the top of the box with her hand. Years of accumulated dust was pushed aside revealing a name scratched into the surface.

"It says *David.* The box must have belonged to him. Let's open it and have a look inside."

"Go ahead," Chuck said. His interest had already faded, and he turned back to work on the wall.

Ginger tried but couldn't get the box opened.

"It's locked."

Chuck reluctantly took a tool from his toolbox to pry the top open.

"You're not going to give me a moment's peace until your curiosity is satisfied. I know you, girl."

The top was preyed open as Ginger waited. Neither of them could foresee the repulsion or the entanglement into the lives of the previous owners and the people of Hemlock Bay that their discovery was about to cause. The top broke free. Together, they lifted the lid of the green toolbox only to gasp in horror.

CHAPTER 33

In late July, the cabin on Butternut Lake was torn down. It was the O'Conner's decision. Ginger claimed that she couldn't stay there. A "For Sale" sign was posted on the lake lot. An unsuspecting couple would venture by later that summer and buy the empty lot for the construction of their dream cabin.

Jeb and Stephanie as well as the town's sheriff, Robert Tucker, insisted that the baby had been a stillbirth.

"All the evidence indicates that the baby was dead before being buried in the toolbox," they said.

"What evidence?" The town had cried.

The State Crime Lab sent an investigation team to help Sheriff Tucker. But their investigation was inconclusive. All that had been left were the skeleton remains in the toolbox.

"The incident is over forty years old," the authorities had said. "It's difficult to piece together a positive conclusion because the parties directly involved are deceased."

Late that night, Minnow Point Hospital admitted a Mr. William Tucker suffering from an apparent heart attack.

"It happened while he was watching the news," the frail lady in the wheelchair told the doctors. "He was fine, just fine, and then he yelled and clutched at his chest."

"Was he disturbed by something on the news?" A nurse asked her.

"He's always disturbed by something on the news."

The authorities in Hemlock Bay, mainly a Mr. Robert Tucker, decided to drop the investigation.

The population of Hemlock Bay, those who were cognizant of the events, were satisfied that the cabin was being torn down and the property would no longer be occupied by Beinfields. The whole incident could now be closed.

The removal of the cabin attracted a small group of onlookers. As the last boards came down, someone in the crowd discovered a message written in pen on a plank of wood that had been inside one of the walls. It was a quote and quite poetic. It sounded familiar to some. But a quote from where, no one knew for sure.

"I think it came from the Bible," one woman stated.

> One generation passeth away, and another generation cometh:
> All the rivers run into the sea: yet the sea is not full
> unto the place from whence the rivers come, thither they return again.

Olivia Beinfield had the last word. No one knew for sure what the words meant. But Olivia did, as she smiled down on all the frenzy below.

ABOUT THE AUTHOR

Barbara Ann Perkins lives in Northern Wisconsin among the pristine lakes and piney forests that are the backdrop for her story. Having given up the North's frosty winters, she now relishes the warm beaches of Florida for a part of each year. Both locations are enjoyed by her along with her husband, Gary, her three grown children and five grandchildren.

Barbara's joy of writing was mainly influenced by two people, her fourth grade teacher who put a premium on creative writing and her father who kept her younger self enthralled on Saturday mornings with his fairy tales.

She has published a number of nonfiction articles, *Astrology for a Skeptic* published in the January 1998 issue of FATE Magazine being her favorite.

Spirits and Secrets is her debut novel. Several items in the story were based on real-life experiences. Anyone familiar with the Wisconsin Northwoods will recognize many of the places mentioned in the story. And the surprise ending, it was on a newscast, as it really happened, somewhere!

CPSIA information can be obtained
at www.ICGtesting.com
Printed in the USA
BVHW081024040423
661729BV00002BA/232

9 781638 142546